DÁL RIADA
FOLK TALES

DÁL RIADA
FOLK TALES

COLIN URWIN

ILLUSTRATED BY
EILEEN-MARIE EMERSON

The
History
Press

Dedicated to the memory of my father,
Ray Urwin (1923–1982)

First published 2025

The History Press
97 St George's Place, Cheltenham,
Gloucestershire, GL50 3QB
www.thehistorypress.co.uk

Typesetting and origination by The History Press
Printed and bound in Great Britain by TJ Books, Padstow, Cornwall.

EU Authorised Representative: Easy Access System Europe
Mustamäe tee 50, 10621 Tallinn, Estonia
gpst.request@easproject.com

Contents

Acknowledgements

Heartfelt thanks go to my wife, Carol, for her continued support during long evenings when I remove myself to read and write, or when I am away somewhere telling stories and singing songs.

I am also very grateful to the many people who support my creativity and performance career by inviting me to their events, coming along to sit in the audience or purchasing my books and recordings.

Numerous people have assisted in so many small ways to see the completion of this project, answering questions, translating Irish and Scots Gaelic, and just enquiring how I was getting on. I appreciate all your help and encouragement. Special thanks go to Dr David Hume MBE, Ulster-Scots historian, author and broadcaster, who kindly agreed to write the foreword.

I am indebted to Nicola Guy, a commissioning editor at The History Press, and all her colleagues with whom I have worked. It is always a pleasure.

Last, but by no means least, I would like to express my immense gratitude and admiration for the work of E.M. Emerson, artist and illustrator and, I'm pleased and proud to say, friend. Her beautiful art is simply stunning, and I hope readers will appreciate, as I do, the lengths to which she goes to bring an extra layer of magic to the pages of my books.

Foreword

The Belfast poet John Hewitt reflected in his work 'Lost Argo' on the story of a boyhood model yacht that his father bought him and brought to Islandmagee in County Antrim on their summer holidays. In the delight of having the small boat, however, the ebbing tide took it beyond his father's reach at Brown's Bay; opposite the stormy gap, the poet tells us, 'she stalled, shivered and headed out, as if enthralled by the far prospect of the Scottish shores'.

The prospect of the Scottish shores similarly enthralled me, growing up on a hillside farm overlooking Islandmagee and the North Channel. On a clear day Portpatrick and the Galloway Hills were visible, the Ailsa Craig further north, and beyond that Kintyre. On a favourable day the Paps of Jura were also part of the panorama. Those Scottish shores were not such a far prospect, 12 miles across at the narrowest point between Torr Head and Kintyre, and just over 20 miles from Portpatrick to the Antrim coast.

The North Channel that divides the two landmasses was more of a communication channel in ancient times than a divide, and although much history has come and gone over centuries, the coastlines of Antrim, Argyll and western Scotland endure. It is also enthralling to me to think of the ancient people who crossed from Antrim to Argyll and eventually formed the Kingdom of Dál Riada that straddled the North Channel. As the legend of Cú Chulainn on Skye (retold in this volume) further shows us, the sea did not divide in any meaningful way.

This common land and seascape has much to offer us by way of legend and history, and Colin Urwin has assembled a remarkable collection of stories from Kintyre, Argyll, the Hebrides, Rathlin Island and the Glens of Antrim. There are stories of fairies, banshees, of the Ulster warrior Cú Chulainn, of Robert the Bruce, swans, seals, witches, the 'Devil's Buttermilk' and much more. Colin has taken these stories and added his own unique imprint to them, preserving them for a new readership and future generations.

I was particularly taken by the story of 'The Kintyre Fox'. It is remarkably similar to the story of 'Tod's Rodden' on Islandmagee. Both have as their central feature a cunning fox that has learned to use a hanging branch to swing out of the path of pursuing hounds and get to its den safely. And both have a similar ending. The Islandmagee story was printed in national reading books in Ireland in the nineteenth century (I have my grandfather's copy). Although it would be disappointing to learn that one story might just be a copy of the other, neither should we discount the truth that, just like foxes, storytellers are cunning and clever, and that the two stories might be separate entities. I hope they are.

In this volume of stories can be found common denominators which we all find enthralling; there is drama, suspense, sometimes scary goings on, little people and larger than life heroes. For most, we must suspend our natural belief. The art of the storyteller is to take us smoothly and without question to a different reality that we can believe in. Colin Urwin has produced a wonderful collection of stories. Be enthralled as you journey through the pages of his book!

Dr David Hume MBE
Ulster Scots historian, author and broadcaster
Magheramorne, County Antrim

Introduction

Long before Ireland or Scotland ever developed distinct national identities, what would become Erin and Alba were divided into many smaller kingdoms with local chieftains and kings vying for power and territory. Perhaps the most unusual of these kingdoms was Dál Riada – Dál meaning *portion of* and Riada referring to some long-forgotten clan name or the like (see also Dál Riata or Dalriada).

Said to have been founded in the fifth century by the legendary Gaelic king, Fergus Mór mac Eirc, at one time the territory included what is now north-east County Antrim – the Antrim Glens and along the north coast to include Rathlin Island. To the north was what is present-day Argyll, from Kintyre up through the Western Isles, or Inner Hebrides, to the Isle of Skye.

Swirling in and around this ancient kingdom and her many islands and countless miles of rugged coastline was the restless waters of the Sea of Moyle – the north channel where the Atlantic Ocean meets the Irish Sea – and what is now the Sea of the Hebrides. Far from being a barrier, the sea connected every part of the kingdom. Only one good day's sailing separated Skye from the southern Antrim Glens, the two furthest points. The widest sea crossing was between the Antrim and Kintyre coasts, which is little over 12 miles at the closest point. A journey of this distance was easier to undertake and less perilous over water than through thickly wooded countryside full of wild boar, red stags and wolves, not to mention bands of potentially hostile clansmen.

It is suggested that the islands and hinterland of the Argyll coast were raided and later settled by a tribe of Gaels from the Irish side of the north Channel. Indeed, Argyll literally means Coast of the Gael. This tribe was known to Greek and Roman writers as the Scoti. Some historians have suggested that the Scoti were to the Gaels what the Vikings were to the Norse – seafaring warriors and pirate raiders. In any case, the Scoti subsequently gave their name to Scotia – Scotland – but that was not for several centuries to come.

Like all the smaller kingdoms that once existed throughout the islands of Ireland and Britain, their borders were in constant flux and their rulers always under threat. Dál Riada did not last as long as some others. It flourished and declined within three or four centuries, though scholars debating the exact details of its rise and fall are far from agreed. Suffice to say, it is a complex historical conundrum involving complicated genealogies and scant archaeological or documentary evidence to prove or disprove any one theory, timeline or set of events.

What is not in dispute, however, is that despite recognised federal borders being in place this long many centuries, and strong national traits and identities firmly established on either side of the Sea of Moyle, the people of what was once the kingdom of Dál Riada share a common Gaelic heritage. Ulster Irish, for example, and especially the dialect once spoken on Rathlin Island, bears closer correlation to the Scots Gaelic of the west coast than Irish spoken anywhere else on the island of Ireland. Latterly, accents and dialects of English heard throughout the region, often impenetrable to outsiders, are easily understood across the board.

I have had a lifelong interest in the local Glens of Antrim history, myths and legends and I am constantly reminded of how the folklore, music and stories of this part of County Antrim are intertwined with those of the Hebridean Islands and Argyll. I think it is all but beyond doubt that many of the people now living in what was the ancient Kingdom of Dál Riada share ancestral, historical and cultural roots. These connections long pre-date the Plantation of Ulster in the seventeenth century, largely by Scottish settlers.

It is well documented that the McDonnells of Antrim are direct descendants of the twelfth-century Hiberno-Norse Warrior Somerled, and for 400 hundred years the clan were Lords of the Isles with strongholds, most notably on Islay and the Antrim coast. That people have been travelling back and forth across the sea between Ireland and Scotland for centuries is also evidenced throughout the Antrim Glens by the prevalence of family names like McAllister, McKeegan, McKinley, McAuley, and so forth.

From the misty Isle of Skye to the beautiful Glens of Antrim and everywhere in between, I have had the great pleasure of travelling through the islands and western highlands. It has been my experience that, in the main, the local people are possessed of identifiable, inherent characteristics: a love of the land and the natural world, hard-working, welcoming and warm (once you get by an initial reserve), loyal and loving to their own, and always up for a bit of craic – be it music, song or story.

As a traveller, I always feel as much at home in some far-flung Hebridean island as I do in the Glens of Antrim where I live. As a storyteller and a singer, I am most comfortable telling stories and singing songs that embrace the history and folklore and landscapes and people that I know best. By extension I include the rest of what was Dál Riada simply because it feels so culturally familiar to me.

In this collection I have tried to find interesting stories that reflect the diversity of folklore to be found throughout the region. Sadly, because of the limitations of this book, I have not been able include all of the many fascinating snippets of lore and legend I have come across. From faerie mice on Rhum to an imprisoned ghostly Norse maiden on Canna and many more fantastical creatures and characters, there is literally a story to be found on every rocky islet and in every locality, however small or remote.

As always, some places have yielded more than others either because of geography, local history, size of population or a combination of these factors. An island like Skye, with its ancient past, spectacularly mountainous landscapes and relatively large population, is obviously going to deliver more folklore than somewhere like Jura, for example, with a small number of inhabitants and a less-prominent historical role, beautiful and interesting as it is. Of course, it also depends on whether early collectors took an interest in a particular place or not, and if their stories were recorded or died out due to the migration of people or the encroachment of the modern world.

In my quest to find material I have combed through many older collections and reference books (for my full list see the sources section at the end of this book). We are all indebted to those who had the foresight to collect these stories and folklore first-hand, often in the old Gaelic, and set them down in print. Generally, debate still smoulders among storytellers, writers and academics about the ethics and value of writing down stories from the oral tradition. In a world that values oral storytelling much less than it once did, it is, in my opinion, essential to preserve these stories in whatever way we can and make them available to as wide an audience as possible.

The alternative is to risk the loss of these precious folk tales and all the beauty and wisdom that goes along with them. I do not subscribe to the view that I have heard espoused by some, that once a story is written down it somehow dies. How could that be? Written down, the words are there to be pored over and, filtered through the reader's imagination, to delight and inspire. From the page they can be lifted, reimagined and retold at any time by anyone. It does not go without saying, however, that the storyteller must pay all due respect to the folkloric conventions of the culture from which the story has come. This was unconsciously intrinsic to tellers of the oral tradition but could be easily and innocently overlooked when working from written source material.

In any case, the folk tales in this anthology have already been written down in some form another, and in some cases hundreds of years ago. For my part, I have felt the need to rework every story to a lesser or greater degree, whether to make the archaic language more accessible, or the narrative flow better, or simply to breathe new energy into the story by way of a little judicious creativity. For this I make no apology. My brief was to reimagine and rework these old stories to suit the tastes of a modern audience. I believe this continuous process keeps the stories alive, interesting and relevant to successive generations of storytellers and students of folklore. Besides, it is my strong conviction that every storyteller must imbue the tale they are telling with their own personality and style, while at the same time – and it's worth mentioning again – staying true to the tradition. This is what I have endeavoured to do and, I hope, achieved.

The researching and writing of this book has, as always, been very satisfying, but the sheer joy and excitement of revisiting many of the spectacular land and seascapes from which the stories originate is always tremendously emotional and special. This is especially so for me when I visit the Western Isles because I have fond memories of my father reminiscing about the Sea of the Hebrides and her many beautiful islands and moods. His ship patrolled these waters during the latter half of the Second World War, training the Atlantic convoy escort groups, meeting incoming convoy ships and guiding them to the safer waters of the Irish Sea, and hunting lonewolf U-boats.

Today, standing on the cliff tops at Fairhead looking out across the swirling sound to Rathlin; or wandering among the grassy sand dunes on Islay listening to the myriad voices of geese and swans; or catching glimpses of eagles and otters on the wild Isle of Mull; or getting up close to whales in the rich waters around the Tresnish Islands; or imagining the presence of monks and Vikings among the ancient ruins of Iona; or scrambling up rugged mountain tracks to discover breathtaking views in the mighty Cuillins of Skye are all grand and wonderful experiences.

I hope some of that wonder comes through in these old stories. I hope, too, that readers might feel the urge to come and visit some of these hauntingly beautiful places and feel a little of the magic for themselves. Perhaps some will even be inspired to retell one or two of these old and enchanting stories to a rapt audience in a bothy some evening by the light of candle or over a wee dram of whisky. *Sláinte ...*

Colin Urwin
Glenarm
December 2024

SKYE

1. Sgáithach and Cú Chulainn

This story forms part of the Ulster or Red Branch Cycle: a collection of medieval Irish heroic legends and sagas that is one of the four cycles of Irish mythology. Mainly featuring the Uliad and the mythical Ulster king, Conchobar mac Nessa, enthroned at Emain Macha, and Cú Chulainn, the warrior-hero endowed with superhuman powers, it first appears in written form in Lebor na hUidre – Book of the Dun Cow, *c.1106, and later the Book of Leinster, c.1160. The stories are thought by some, however, to be up to five or more centuries older than this.*

This version is compiled from various sources including that found in Otto F. Swire's book, Skye, The Island and its Legends *(Blackie & Son Limited, Glasgow, 1961).*

Sgáithach, which means Shadow in the old Gaelic, was an ancient warrior queen. Some even say she was a goddess possessed of the power to convey brave warriors killed in battle to Tír na nÓg – Land of the Forever Young. She was known to be undefeated in battle and was famous throughout the lands of the Gael and far beyond. Exactly when she came to dwell among the wild rugged mountains of the island that would bear her name is not known, but come to the Isle of Skye she did.

She chose as her residence a place near Tarskavaig on the south-west coast of Skye. It was and still is unequalled for its raw beauty and commanding views over the sea. Here she built a fort known as Dún Sgáith – Fortress of Shadow. She founded a school where warriors, already proven in battle, could study for a year and become even more practised in certain martial arts. They learned how to vault over the walls of fortresses using only a hazel pole, how to fight underwater and, finally, how to take up and use Sgáithach's deadly barbed throwing spear, the Gáe Bulg. Many proved themselves unworthy and did not survive, for the training was even more fierce than any real battle.

Perhaps Sgáithach's most famous student was the great hero and guardian of Ulster, Cú Chulainn. His reputation as a fearless and ferocious warrior was unrivalled. He defeated whole armies single-handedly, and it was said that after battle three ice cold vats of water had to be prepared for him. When he immersed himself in the first it evaporated as steam, the second boiled over like a pot on an untended fire and the third came to an agreeable temperature fit to wash the blood and sweat from his body.

But let us not run ahead of the story. Before all this, Cú Chulainn fell in love with Emer, the beautiful daughter of an Ulster chieftain. Emer's father, Forgall, disapproved of the match and only agreed to their marriage on the condition that Cú Chulainn would enter training as a warrior with Sgáithach. In his heart of hearts, he hoped his daughter's young suitor would fail and never return. But Cú Chulainn was born to be a hero.

To begin with, Sgáithach all but ignored the strange upstart youngster who had travelled with his compatriots over the sea from Ulster. To impress her, Cú Chulainn soon attracted trouble and tempest like moths to a flame. In a spirited mock fight that lasted two days and nights, Cú Chulainn accidentally broke the fingers of Sgáithach's warrior daughter, Uathach. She cried out in pain and her suitor, Cochar Croibhe, ran to her side. Seeing her injured, and to prove his abiding love, he challenged Cú Chulainn to a duel of single combat. Uathach protested, but the die was cast. Cú Chulainn easily defeated Cochar Croibhe and slew him without mercy.

To make up for this misdeed, Cú Chulainn offered to shoulder Cochar Croibhe's responsibilities, but he soon became Uathach's lover, apparently forgetting all about Emer, his betrothed back in Ulster. Eventually, Sgáithach was compelled to promise her daughter to Cú Chulainn and, perhaps feeling a sense of loyalty to his future mother-in-law, or to gain her approval further, he challenged Sgáithach's fearsome rival sister, Aífe. Making use of little distracting lies, he defeated her in combat. With the blade of his sword at her throat, he demanded Aífe cease hostilities with her sister forthwith and, as if to seal the bargain, to allow him to impregnate her. In return for her life, Aífe agreed and later gave birth to Cú Chulainn's son, Connla – but this is another chapter of a very long story.

Greatly displeased with Cú Chulainn, Sgáithach descended from Dún Sgáith in a violent rage and challenged him to combat herself.

'Come and learn all ye heroes,' she cried, 'for never will ye see the likes of this again.'

Then the two mighty warriors clashed. They fought for three days and three nights over mountain, moor and marsh, but neither could gain the upper hand.

Uathach could see that her mother meant to fight to the death if necessary. She called for some sour hind's milk and made the crowdie cheese that was her mother's favourite. She baked a loaf and wafted the pleasant smell of the fresh, warm bread in the direction of the two combatants. She begged them to leave off their fighting and to come and refresh themselves, but they were like two red deer stags with their antlers locked in battle.

Then Uathach called for a fresh salmon. She cooked it over an open fire until the flesh was pink and moist and so tender that it fell from the bones. The skin was golden brown and crisp, and the smell so delicious that wolves salivated and howled for miles around. But neither Cú Chulainn nor Sgáithach would relent.

At last, Uathach roasted a wild boar on a spit. She stuffed it with hazelnuts gathered from the trees that grew by a burn on the side of a hill called Broc-Bheinn. The nuts were long known to be the source of great wisdom to anyone who ate them. As soon as the smell of those roasting hazelnuts reached the nostrils of Cú Chulainn and Sgáithach it came to them both in the same instant that if they ate of those nuts they would gain the knowledge and wisdom to overcome any rival. And so, they agreed to lay down their arms and take a little refreshment.

At first they ignored the salmon and the bread and the cheese. They even ignored the wild boar. They went straight to the hazelnuts, and the moment they ate them both warriors realised that neither would ever get the better of the other in combat.

They rose from their meal sated and, to everyone's surprise, they did not pick up their weapons. Instead, they kissed and embraced one another. Between them they made a solemn promise of peace. They swore that if ever one needed the other's help then all they had to do was ask and it would be given, 'Even,' they vowed, 'if the heavens should fall and we be crushed.'

It is often whispered that Sgáithach took Cú Chulainn as her lover that night. But soon afterwards Cú Chulainn had to return to Ulster, where his exploits became, quite literally, the stuff of legend. Sgáithach remained on the Isle of Skye for the rest of her long life, but an unbreakable bond had been formed between her and Cú Chulainn.

Whether or not one ever called on the other for help, no one really knows. All I can tell you is that as a mark of respect and the deep affection Sgáithach bore for her ally and, perhaps, lover, she called the mountains of Skye Cú Chulainn's Hills in his memory. And that is the name they bear to this very day.

2. The Swan Maiden of Skye

This remarkable and heart-rending story was found in Otto F. Swire's The Inner Hebrides and their Legends *(Collins, London and Glasgow, 1964). Caught between two worlds, the child is a damned soul and even today this story is bound to resonate with any individual or group of people who find themselves in a comparable situation.*

There are similar stories where some otherworldly female entity agrees to marry a mortal man but only on certain conditions. The male character seems always bound to fail to keep the conditions or promises he makes but we cannot help wishing that he will succeed. This story is, in my opinion, among the very best and most beautiful of that genre.

Many centuries ago, down near the little sheltered bay of Gesto in the west of Skye, there lived a handsome young fisherman called Hamish. Day after day he went out in his currach like the other men. When all around were hauling in the good eating fish like cod and mackerel and herring, his net was empty but for dogfish and bony wrasse.

One evening, as he was returning home yet again with little to show for all his labours, he cursed his luck at the top of his lungs and vowed never to return to the sea. Just then he saw something glowing in the gathering dusk. It was like the light of a silvery moon behind a whisp of cloud slowly coming towards him over the water. Mesmerised, Hamish stood up in his currach. As he did so the strange light slowly took the shape of the most beautiful young maiden he could have ever imagined. She was clad all in flowing white. Her skin was just as pale and her long hair had a soft flaxen tint. The only other colours in this pale vision of a woman were the rosy-red of her lips and her eyes as black as ink.

Hamish was completely spellbound by the young maiden, so beautiful and strange was she. But before he could gather his thoughts or feel any kind of fear she spoke to him.

'Hamish I beg you, do not give up your fishing. Come back to the sea and I promise good fortune will follow you.'

With that the vision of the maiden faded from view and was gone. From that moment onwards Hamish cared not whether he caught any fish or went hungry. All he could think of was the young woman. Every waking hour he ached for her and little he slept dreaming about her, such was his burning desire.

Each and every day he went out fishing, but always he searched for her and hoped she would appear again.

Hamish began to prosper as his luck turned and many a young maid round and about kept her eye on him. Any one of them would have gladly taken him for a husband, but one lassie had long set her heart on him and let it be known that she meant to have Hamish come hell or high water. Anyone with half an eye could see how she flirted with him and dallied around him, but he was blind to her attentions.

This day Hamish went out in his currach from Gesto Bay to where he had first seen the maiden. When he was far from land, he laid up his oars. No fishing did he undertake. He just sat there, rocked by the gentle waves, searching the horizon and waiting for darkness to come as he drifted with the tide. Eventually, when his passion and pulse was racing with the fever of desire, he stood up in his currach and with his arms outspread he called out to her.

'Oh, beautiful white maiden, please show yourself to me. I am sick for the love of thee. I would rather die than live my life without you.'

With that, Hamish made to step over the gunwale of his currach into the water. As he did so he suddenly caught sight of a swan pushing itself with great speed through the water towards him. It came alongside and Hamish stepped out onto its back. Gracefully, the huge bird carried him to shore. The moment the swan touched land it took the form of the beautiful young maiden, and she began to speak breathlessly.

'I could not come to you again, Hamish, until you proved that your love for me was stronger than your fear of death. Now may I declare my love for you. My heart was broken that night you vowed never to return to the sea again. I had to show myself to you. Now I can stay with you in my mortal form forever.'

Hamish and the young woman were locked in each other's arms for a long time.

'Will you marry me?' he whispered.

'We can be married, but you must promise me something first.'

'Anything, my love. I will do anything for you.'

'Never must you ask my name or from where I have come. Promise me this.'

Well, Hamish was so in love with the swan maiden that he would have promised her the Earth and the moon and the stars.

'I swear on the graves of our unborn children, I will die before I break my promise to thee,' he said, and she willingly took him at his word.

Hamish and the maiden were married, and never were a couple so blissfully happy or so in love with one another. They were joined at the hip, and never did an unpleasant word passed between them.

Time passed and soon Hamish and his wife were blessed with a child. The baby boy was the sweet fruit of their love together and neither could have been happier. Most people wished them well, but not so the young woman who had wanted to marry Hamish. She was consumed by jealousy and at every opportunity she cast slurs on Hamish's wife and dripped poison into the ear of anyone who would listen. One day she contrived to meet Hamish down by the shore as he worked at his currach.

'How sad for that wee laddie of yours that he'll never know his mother's name or where on this Earth he came from,' she said carelessly.

'Of course he will know,' answered Hamish, suddenly angered by her words.

'How can he, when his mother has played you for a fool while she keeps all her secrets and makes you keep your promise?' she spat.

Having planted the seed, the woman walked away, content with her work.

Hamish pondered the words all day while he toiled, and as he did he became more and more aggrieved at the seeming injustice of his wife's conditions on their love. When he came home from fishing that evening he was in a dark mood.

'I have been thinking, wife,' he said at their supper table, 'how unfair it is that you keep all these secrets from me, and now our son too. How is he to grow up not knowing his mother's name or from where she came?'

'Hamish, before we were married you swore that you would die before breaking your promise,' said his wife, with her lips trembling.

'Aye well, that was then, this is now. No son of mine will be reared not knowing who his mother is or even her name,' Hamish roared, and he banged his fist on the table.

Hamish's wife rose from the table. She lifted her child from the cradle and departed without another word. All that she left on the covers of their bed was a single white swan's feather.

When the temper was off him, Hamish hunted for her high up and low down, but never again did he see her or hear tell of her. How he regretted his words and how bitterly he regretted breaking his promise. What was done was done, however, and Hamish bore his loss like a terrible grief. The people felt some pity for him, for they knew that Hamish's wife was not of this world but some faerie woman of the sea who had, they said, beguiled him.

In time Hamish remarried, for he was a lonely man. His second wife was a fine housekeeper and companion, but she could never love him as the swan maiden had, nor could he give himself to her so completely as he had done to his first wife. Even so, together they were to have a child. When her time came a local henwife was summoned to help with the delivery. Always mindful of the faerie folk's conniving ways at these tenderest of times, and knowing of Hamish's past with the faerie woman, the henwife took every precaution against otherworldly interference. Horseshoes and fire tongs and all manner of iron-made implements were set out, and wreaths of rowan twigs were made and hung about the place.

That night, as Hamish's wife lay on the bed nursing her newborn, a glowing vision came to her. It was that of a beautiful young woman. She was clad all in flowing white. Her skin was a just as pale and her long hair had a soft flaxen tint. In the woman's arms was a little child. She came close and made to offer the infant to Hamish's wife. The poor woman was petrified and held up a rowan wreath to ward the evil away and the vison faded from view. On the bed covers was found a single white swan's feather.

Hamish's wife did not tell her husband what she had seen, for she knew who the faerie woman was and that the child she bore was her husband's firstborn. But she did tell the henwife and all care was taken to guard against any more otherworldly visits.

Hamish's wife went on to have many more children, and after every birth it was the same. Faithfully, the vision of the beautiful young faerie woman would appear, offering her child, but Hamish's wife always refused. After every visitation there would be a single white swan's feather left on the bed covers.

Let it be true or false, it is said that since then, whenever any descendant of Hamish the fisherman is born, a single pure white swan's feather is always found on the bedclothes the following morning.

And folk may wonder why the swan maiden would want to give up her child to a human wet nurse. Like all mothers, she only wants what is best for her child. You see, those poor children, half-human and half-faerie, are shunned in the otherworld. They become graceless, discontented creatures, damned for all eternity to search for a place to call home. The quetion is, would they be any less shunned in our world?

3. The Sea Cattle of Skye

All along the western seaboard of Ireland and Scotland are found numerous tales of cattle coming up from the sea to graze on land, sometimes to lure land cattle away, sometimes to bring good fortune to some luckless or impoverished farmer. Indeed, in Ireland the origins of all cattle are attributed to such beasts.

This short account is compiled from a number of sources, most notably sketches on the subject contained in Alisdair Alpin McGregor's book The Peat Fire Flame *(The Moray Press, Edinburgh & London, 1937).*

In the far north-west of Skye, upon a time now long forgotten, there were herds of cattle kept at Monkstadt near Uig and further north at Duntulm on the Trotternish peninsula. The animals were said to be so beautiful and even-tempered that they must have had the blood of sea cattle in them. And who knows, for they very well might have.

Rare it was for sea cattle to come ashore. But sometimes, late on summer evenings, they came to graze on the sweet, salt-laden grasses and aromatic herbs, perhaps as a change from their usual fare of seaweed.

Once a herd landed up on the shore near the Great Rock of McNicol at Scorribreac farm overlooking Portree bay. The Nicolson clansmen, who were said to be of Norse kinship, raised a low earthen ditch to block the cattle's return path to the strand, for it was believed that they would not cross bare earth. Perhaps if they had sprinkled soil taken from some nearby burial place – that is to say, consecrated ground – which was said to work much better, they might have prevented the cattle from returning to the ocean.

As it was, sometime later the voice of a faery herdswoman was heard gently calling her kine in a strange but beautiful singing rhyme:

Crooked one,
Dun one,
Little wing,
Grizzled.
Black cow,
White cow,
Little bull,
Black-headed one.
My milch kine have come home,
O dear!
That the herdsman would come!

One by one the faery beasts lifted their heads and lowed in answer to their names. They left off their grazing and obediently followed one after the other, easily skipping over the earthen barrier set to hold them back. They returned to their home beyond the waves and this world, never to be seen again.

4. The Three Faerie Women

In The Peat Fire Flame, *McGregor refers to the ghostly women in this old Isle of Skye story as Banshees. Banshee (*bean sí *or* bean sídhe*) literally means faerie woman. In the folklore of Ireland, the* bean sídhe *exclusively heralds the death of a member of certain families or clans.* Caoineag *or* caointeach *perform a similar role in Scottish folklore. In McGregor's version, I think, the term 'banshee' is used more generally, for want of a specific term, to refer to a different class of faerie women, that is, those who abduct human children and sometimes leave changelings or lifeless substitutes.*

This is a dark tale of a type that may have come about to help ration-alise child mortality and other sudden or unexplained deaths. For those struggling to come to terms with their grief, these kinds of stories may have brought some little comfort.

Many years ago, in the wild west of the Isle of Skye where the great Black Cuillins rise up stark and jagged from the sea, there lived a shepherd by the name of MacSwain. He worked to a tacksman, who leased a vast acreage of grazing from the local laird and kept a great flock of sheep in the locality of Glen Brittle. As might be imagined, MacSwain was never off the go, especially at lambing time when for a month and more he barely slept at all. But such was the hard life of a shepherd in those bygone days.

One year his wife, Annie, gave birth to their third child – a baby girl. The other two had died in their wee cribs when they were but a few days old. MacSwain was busy with the lamb-ing and was not able to spare a moment to care for his wife and newborn child. Thankfully, a kindly neighbour came in for a day or two to nurse Annie, for she was poorly enough following the delivery.

One day, when the neighbour had the wee cottage shining like a new pin and the peats were burning away on the hearth and the kettle simmering by the hob, she thought she would lift the child herself – just to hold her for a wee while.

'There now,' she said to Annie, 'let me take the bairn and you get some rest yourself.' And she lifted the child and began crooning away as she rocked it gently in her arms.

Well, any mother will tell you that for the first few months of their child's life they don't know what sleep is. No matter how tired they become, they are always attentive to the slightest stirrings of their baby, and so it was with Annie. She lay back on her pillows and closed her eyes. She even drifted off into a kind of half sleep, though she could still hear the neighbour softly crooning and the burning peats whispering away.

A sort of a calm came over the household. With the heat of the fire and all the work she had done, the neighbour woman's eyes became very heavy and she yawned wearily. Eventually she fell fast asleep in the chair, with the child dead to the world in her arms. But then some sense of danger brought Annie to the alert! Her whole body tensed as she cracked opened her eyes a little and instinctively squinted in the direction of her child. What she saw filled her very bones with an icy dread.

Standing by the fire overlooking the neighbour woman and the child were three strange, wraith-like old hags. They were some class of *bean sídhe* or witches, thought Annie.

'Take the child and our business here will be done,' cackled the first one.

'Ah Sister, have you not had enough of this woman's children?' mocked the second.

'Leave her this runt a while. We can come back for her another time,' said the third.

Well, the first old woman ranted and raged and with her long bony finger she pointed to an ember of peat smouldering on the hearth.

'You see that *caoron* there? By the time that has burned away this child will be mine.' And with a swirl of mist and cold air the three old hags disappeared up the chimney and away back to the faerie world or wherever they came from.

Having been robbed of two bairns already, Annie wasn't about to lose her third without a fight. Weak as she was, the poor woman raised herself from the bed and with the fire tongs she lifted that peat out of the fire and doused it in the kettle of water sitting by the hob. While the neighbour and her baby slept, Annie wrapped the remains of the charred peat in a piece of linen and buried it at the bottom of the kist under blankets and shawls and her own wedding dress.

Time passed, eighteen years in fact, and Annie's baby girl grew into a fine young woman. She was the rose of Glen Brittle. Her name was Oighrig, and it wasn't too long before local lads came looking for her hand, and it wasn't very long after that she was betrothed.

In those far off days it was the custom for brides-to-be to stay away from their place of worship between the time of their betrothal and their wedding day. On Sunday mornings Oighrig's parents made the 12-mile journey on foot to the parish church at Eynort and left their daughter to her chores and her own devices.

As the wedding day approached Oighrig became more and more excited, and one Sunday morning after her parents had left for church, she went down into the room and opened the kist. She took out her mother's wedding dress and tried it on. It fitted perfectly and Oighrig gazed at herself in a looking glass and held up her long tresses admiringly.

Many of us have been guilty of plundering, and sure once the kist was open Oighrig couldn't help herself. She delved deeper into the box to see what other treasures her mother kept there. There were blankets and shawls and a few coloured ribbons. There were a few more little keepsakes, and right at the bottom was something bound up in a piece of dirty old linen. Oighrig unwrapped it and to her puzzlement found it was a small piece of blackened peat. 'What on earth would mother keep an old lump of burnt peat for?' she said to herself. For the life of her Oighrig could not imagine.

Anyhow, she decided to tidy out the kist, and the first thing she did was to throw the lump of peat, rag and all, onto the fire. As she worked she became very tired and lightheaded, and eventually so weak she fell to the floor. She tried to drag herself towards the half door and into God's daylight, but all strength had left her.

The last earthly sounds Oighrig heard were her parents arriving home and the shriek of her mother as she took all in and called her daughter's name. In an instant Annie McSwain doused the fire with the kettle, but alas it was too late. The stub of peat had burned away and a pale shadow of Oighrig lay motionless on the floor.

For eighteen years Annie McSwain had outwitted the old women of the *sídhe*, but in the end they took her daughter. Not even Annie's husband believed her when she said the faerie folk had taken Oighrig and left a lifeless changeling in her place. She begged the people not to bury the unholy thing in the parish graveyard at Eynort, but no one listened to her, for they thought she had lost her mind with grief.

Only when Annie died herself a few months later, of a broken heart they said, and the family grave was reopened did the people realise Annie had not gone mad after all. Oighrig's body, so carefully wrapped in a shroud and laid in the ground, was not there. In its place lay a gnarled and twisted bough of bog oak wrapped in linen. To what otherworld young Oighrig had been taken no one even dared to imagine.

5. The Widow of Loch Mor

The water horse appears in folklore all over Ireland as the capaill uisce *and in Scotland most often as the kelpie. It is interesting to note that in McGregor's* The Peat Fire Flame *he refers to the creatures as water horses or in the Scots Gaelic as an* each uisge – *as opposed to kelpie. I'm not sure if this suggests that there is a fine distinction between the two, or that the water spirits of the Western Isles are more akin to the Irish variety.*

Most often these creatures of whatever hue attempt to lure young women down into their otherworldly domain beneath the waters of some nearby dark loch, which is almost always a body of fresh water, occasionally a river. In this account the water horse seems to have similar motives but shows more compassion.

Out to the west of Skye under the shadow of Bhatairsteinn (Vaterstein Head) by the shore of Loch Mor is as lonely and bleak a place as can be imagined. Here there once lived a poor old widow woman. She had an unmarried daughter living with her who was her only company and joy in this world. The daughter was full of life and devoted herself to the care of her mother. But the daughter suddenly took ill and over a long time she mysteriously declined. The old woman tried every charm and remedy but eventually the daughter died, leaving her mother to grieve alone.

So heartbroken was the old woman that she could not find the wherewithal to have her daughter buried. Night after night she sat in the tiny hovel of a cabin by her lifeless daughter's side. With nothing but the faint glow of the peats to light the place, sometimes she thought she saw her daughter's breast rise and fall, but alas it was only her imagination playing evil tricks on her.

As a cold winter spell set in, the short days and long nights seemed darker and ever more dreary. During the wee hours the poor old woman thought about dragging herself down to the shore of Loch Mor and wading into the dark waters, but she could not leave her daughter – not even to bring in peats for the fire or to make herself a bite to eat.

One night as she sat there still grieving the loss of her daughter in the almost pitch black, she heard the faint sound of her latch lifting and the creak of the door. A stranger let himself into the house. The old woman was so weak and disinterested in life that she barely lifted her head to take notice and only sensed his presence. Without saying a word, he took up a seat opposite her by the slowly dying fire. Just as it looked as if the last glow of the peats might turn to grey ash, the stranger touched the hearth with his staff and said, '*O caoron, dean solus.*' (O little peat, make a light.)

Immediately the ashes flared up as if the fire had been stoked with fresh peat. In the shadowy light the old woman saw that the stranger was dressed in heavy, dark robes with a hood drawn up over his head. Underneath his robes she saw that his boots were more like the cracked and long neglected hooves of a heavy horse. All night long the stranger stayed with the woman, but never another word was spoken. Just before the first faint light of a misty dawn began to appear, the stranger left.

That morning kindly neighbours from across the glen came and found the old woman. She was near death and rambling wildly. They rekindled the fire and spooned warm broth into her. They asked the whereabouts of her daughter, but not a single word of sense could they get from the old woman. She told them about the dark stranger and in their fear the neighbours sent for a priest. But the oldest and wisest among them said that the house had been visited by the *Each Uisge* – the water horse of Loch Mor. When the ground round about the cabin was searched for signs of its presence, impressed into the soft peaty soil were found the unmistakable imprints of horse's hooves.

They say the water horse of Loch Mor is still under those dark waters where he has lived since time began, only rarely revealing himself to human eyes. What became of the old woman's daughter was the subject of great wonder at ceilidhs for years to come.

'She must have taken her own life,' some ventured.

'Aye, and why wouldn't she? Living out there, and no company but her oul doting mother,' others chimed in.

'Taken she was, by the *Each Uisge*. That's what happened her,' said those with the longest memories of the old stories.

Around many a hearth fire long into the night the folk conjured up their own worst fears. They despaired at their own bleak conclusions and shivered at thoughts of walking home in the dark for, of course, no one knew when or to whom the water horse of Loch Mor would show himself again.

6. The Three Black Cats

As in other places, there are numerous stories in the folklore of Skye featuring black cats, and of 'witches' who can transform themselves into cats. I think these female entities are better viewed as faerie women as opposed to actual women who, as it were, practiced the dark arts. The term witch is loaded with prejudice and the history of female persecution and injustice under this label is dark and disturbing.

The makings of this story came from McGregor's The Peat Fire Flame *and other sources, from which I developed this slightly less dark narrative. The innocent young character central to the version found in McGregor's book meets with a gruesome end that, in my view, is uncalled for. To say the least, it did not provide a very satisfying conclusion to the story for me and others to whom I told it.*

I hope the ending here is a little more heart-warming while retaining a strong element of the macabre. I take this liberty safe in the knowledge that any re-teller of the tale can revert to the earlier version according to their own tastes.

Between Dunvegan and Vaternish in the north-west of the Isle of Skye is a lonely, desolate moor. A narrow stony road runs through the wild country and once, many years ago, a young boy was waylaid there. His name was Ian, and he was only about 12 years old at the time. Everyone thought of him as one of the nicest young fellows you could imagine – always smiling and happy, and always very mannerly.

One day his mother sent him on an errand to his grandparents, who dwelt along the road to Vatnerish. Their cabin was only a few miles away, but it was far from any other habitation. It would have been hard to find, but Ian had been there many times before. What made this journey so special for him was that, for the first time, he was making it on his own. He was bursting with excitement as he set out. He ran almost the whole way never hardly stopping, except once for a pee by the side of the road.

When Ian got to his grandparents' dwelling, of course, they were delighted to see him. Nothing would do but for his grandmother to set him down to a feed of oatmeal porridge. By the time he had eaten his fill and told them all the news from Dunvegan, it was getting late.

'You better get away son, if you want to be home before dark,' said his grandfather as he peered out over the half door.

So, the grandmother kissed and hugged her wee grandson and sent him on his way with a lump of bread in his pocket.

'Straight home now,' said she as Ian took his leave.

Well, with his belly full and him getting tired, Ian did not run home. He dillydallied and every bird and every wee beast caught his eye. It got later and later and darker and darker. Coming up behind him was a big, glowering, grey sky and before Ian knew it hailstones were bouncing off the back of his head. As luck would have it, there was an old, abandoned cabin nearby and he ran to take shelter from the squall.

The cabin hadn't been lived in for a good number of years and the roof was falling in. The door was hanging on one hinge, and the chimney breast was beginning to crumble. Still and all, Ian snuggled up in a nook by the old fireplace and before long he fell fast asleep. I don't know how long he slept, but when he awoke it was pitch black in the old place and he was shivering from the cold.

After a while, Ian's eyesight began to adjust to the darkness, and through a hole in the roof he could see the moon was out. Then he heard a strange meowing noise, like a cat. From the side of his eye, he caught sight of an animal peering in through the hole in the roof, then stealthily dropping down to the floor. It was a great big cat with sleek, jet-black fur and shining green eyes. Suddenly another one just like the first appeared at the opening and came in the same way, and then, low and behold, didn't a third big black cat do the very same.

They rubbed heads with one another the way cats greet their own kind, and they purred and licked each other's black faces. But then suddenly the purring stopped, and before Ian's eyes the cats transformed into three old women who began cackling and laughing and speaking in human voices.

'Some human soul is here,' one of them said cautiously and Ian instinctively closed his eyes tightly and pretended to be asleep.

'There, over by the fireplace,' another of them said. 'It's a boy. What the Devil is he doing here?'

'We'll have to kill him,' said the last one fiercely, 'or he'll betray us.'

Well, Ian was absolutely petrified, but he just kept his eyes closed and never moved a muscle for he knew he was in the presence of great evil.

'It might be better for us to let him live,' said the first one. 'If he truly is sleeping he will not say a word. If he is listening, then he should know that if he betrays us we will come back and tear him to pieces.'

Then, just as mysteriously and suddenly as they appeared, the three old women turned back into big black cats and leapt up and out through the opening in the roof and were gone once more into the night.

It was a long time before Ian gathered the courage to crack open his eyes, first one then the other. When he did so the first grey light of dawn had appeared, and the moon was nearly set. He jumped up and took to his heels. He ran for his life all the way home, but when he got there his mother hadn't even missed him. She thought he had just stayed with his grandparents. She only became suspicious that something was amiss when he refused his breakfast and wouldn't leave her side.

Very soon Ian began to fail. He wasn't sleeping at night, and the young lad's greedy appetite left him entirely. Eventually his mother queried him.

'What's ailing you son? You can tell your mother you know.'

'I can't, Mother,' said he. 'They'll kill me if I do.'

'Kill you! Who will, son?'

'The witches.'

'Witches? What witches, son?'

'Promise you won't tell anyone Mother,' Ian pleaded, 'or they'll kill me.'

'I won't say a word to a living soul.'

And so, Ian relayed the whole story to his mother. Once he'd got it off his chest the young lad began to feel much better. His appetite came back to him, and he got a decent night's sleep for the first time in weeks.

But Ian's mother was so troubled by what he had told her she decided to go to her clergyman for advice. On the way she met a close neighbour and confided in her.

'For heaven's sake keep that to yourself,' she said, but the neighbour told her husband and swore him to secrecy. He told the boys down in Dunvegan. And then the rumours started.

'Did you hear about young Ian?'

'He was near killed by witches.'

'Witches! It must be them that's put the blink on my cow – she hasn't given us a drop of milk in a fortnight.'

And so it went on. By the next day the talk was all over the village. All kinds of mischief, maladies and mayhem were blamed on the witches and fingers started to get pointed, mostly in the wrong direction.

Well, like all these things, the whole affair blew up and died down after a few weeks and the folk soon found other problems to concern them. Ian fretted for the longest, but even he soon put it out of his mind.

Time passed, a year in fact, and Ian turned 13. A little older and wiser, he was sent again on an errand to his grandparents. They were delighted, of course, and they made a great fuss over him, for they hadn't seen hide nor hair of him since his strange ordeal a year before. As nightfall was approaching they sent him on his way with a lump of bread in his pocket.

Dillydallying along the road, Ian was not aware that creeping up behind him were three big cats with glistening, jet-black fur and shining green eyes. As he neared the derelict cottage he happened to glance over his shoulder and spied the stalkers. Quick as lightning, he slipped out of his big heavy coat and ran like a hare to take refuge in the old building. He squeezed into the nook by the fireplace and his eyes went straight up to the opening in the roof.

Sure enough, first one, then two and then a third big black cat crept in and dropped down though that hole. They began to lick each other and purr the way they had done before. Then as one creature, with their heads lowered and their shoulder rising and falling by turns, they started to advance towards their prey.

Just then there was an almighty blast of sparks and smoke, and a withering cloud of hail and dust swept through that old dwelling place. There was an unearthly screeching and a caterwauling the likes of which no man or woman ever heard. Those three black cats disappeared up through that hole in the roof a damn sight quicker than they came down.

When the dust and stour settled, Ian's grandfather was standing there with the barrel of his old fowling piece still smoking.

'Hopefully that's the last we'll ever see of them,' he said to his grandson.

In the years that followed the story got exaggerated and the folk said that Ian was torn to pieces by those cats, but that's not the way of it at all. When he and his grandfather went to retrieve his coat from where he had cast it off along the road they found it in shreds. Maybe that's how the story got embroidered.

Sometime afterwards it was said a cairn was raised to mark the spot where all this happened, and it was whispered that it was haunted – by who or what no one now remembers. As far as I know, that was the last time anyone saw or heard tell of a black cat, a faerie woman or a witch in that part of the Isle of Skye.

7. A Rare Breed

I found the makings of this gem in McGregor's The Peat Fire Flame. *Set on the Isle of Skye, the central female character is portrayed as some kind of witch who uses the young man to go riding around visiting her brethren of an evening. That being the premise, and with such powers, she might just have summoned a horse or used a conventional broom!*

I could not help introducing a slightly more indecent emphasis on the narrative. (See also 'The Breed of the Old Mare'.)

Loch Bracadale is a mighty sea loch lying on the western shore of Skye. Near here a very strange thing occurred one time.

It happened when a young man by the name of Aonghas, who was the favourite retainer of the local tacksman of Ullinish, became entangled in an unfortunate concern.

The tacksman's name was McKinnon and Aonghas was his most trusted and very hardworking assistant. Together they collected the rents and settled disputes between the tenants and looked to the local laird's interests. Aonghas never gave his employer any cause for complaint. In fact, McKinnon looked upon the younger man as his closest confidant. Often it was they shared a meal and a dram or two of whiskey at the end of the day.

As time went by, however, Aonghas began arriving late for his work and became very distracted and lackadaisical in all his tasks. When McKinnon asked if there was anything amiss, Aonghas withheld the reason for his troubling behaviour. As the weeks went by, however, his employer became more and more concerned by the changes in Aonghas' appearance and conduct. His complexion became wan, and his eyes were shot through with blood. The flesh fell from his bones, and he could hardly stay awake for more than five minutes. Then one day he missed his work altogether.

'I demand here and now,' said McKinnon the next morning, 'an explanation as to why you have fallen so low as to miss a day's work and fail so wilfully in your duties.'

'I cannot tell you sir,' said Aonghas.

'You can tell me Aonghas, and you will this instant or as sure as God's in heaven you will be dismissed from my employment without delay.'

Eventually and under considerable duress, Aonghas agreed to tell his employer the whole truth.

'Every night,' started Aonghas, 'when I lie down to sleep I am visited by a woman. She brings with her a bridle, which she places over my head and then puts a spell on me:

'Take this bit in thy mouth
'That I might ride thee north and south
'That I might ride thee east and west
'Afore thou take thy nightly rest.'

McKinnon held his breath, and his eyes were out on stalks as Aonghas continued, but not a word did he utter to interrupt the young man.

'My body is transformed into that of a wild stallion,' continued Aonghas. 'The woman mounts me, and she rides me around the island all night. Before dawn, when I am frothing at the mouth and my flanks are lathered with sweat, she repairs me to my cabin before she undoes the spell:

'Rest ye now my stallion fine
'For soon again thou will be mine
'Take thee now thy human form
'I must away afore the morn.'

When Aonghas had finished his story McKinnon was greatly perturbed and he remained silent for a very long time. Eventually he spoke.

'Never mention a word of this to another living soul,' he said.

'Neither I will,' said Aonghas, 'but what can I do?'

'Tonight, when this witch, or whatever she is, comes, you must be ready. Snatch the bridle from her – you will only have one chance, mind. Use all your strength to place the bridle about her head and turn her own evil words back on her.'

'So I will,' said Aonghas earnestly.

'When she turns into a mare, which if God is good she surely will, take her to the blacksmith and have her shod with iron shoes. Then take her for a gallop around the countryside as hard as ever you can and see if she likes it! Go home now and rest, for you will need all your wits about you.'

As Aonghas left for home, McKinnon called after him.

'Come back here early tomorrow. I will be waiting for news.'

It was a long night, but the next morning Aonghas returned to McKinnon and relayed all he had seen and done.

'When the woman crept into my cabin I was ready for her,' Aonghas said. 'I leapt out of my bed and snatched the bridle from her. Then I put the spell on her:

'Take this bit in thy mouth
'That I might ride thee north and south
'That I might ride thee east and west
'Afore thou take thy nightly rest.'

'Instantly I spoke the words she transformed into a fine grey mare. I jumped on her and I rode her to the blacksmith with great speed, and her screeching and bucking all the way. The blacksmith had to use all his strength and skill to shoe her. Then I jumped upon her once more and rode her away at a gallop. Truth be told, I tired before the mare and while the stars still shone down I dismounted for I was weary. As the mare stood there stamping the ground with her iron shoes, I took pity on her and undid the spell:

'Rest ye now my mare fine
'For ne'er again thou will be mine
'Take thee now thy human form
'I must away afore the morn.

'As I spoke the last word the mare took on the bodily form of a woman once again. She ran away down the track clip-clopping all the way.'

'A blessed night's work laddie,' said McKinnon clapping Aonghas' back. 'Hopefully that's the last we'll see of that accursed witch. And now you can enjoy a peaceful night's sleep and get back to your old self, Aonghas. Now away home and rest, but be back to work bright and early tomorrow.'

Satisfied that his plan had worked so well, McKinnon called for his wife to come into the kitchen that they might breakfast together while he told her of all the strange goings on. When she did not appear, McKinnon went to her chamber. The curtains were drawn, and Mrs McKinnon was still abed. She was moaning and groaning with some strange malady. Her husband sent straight away for a neighbouring henwife. She examined Mrs McKinnon and was flabbergasted to find that the poor woman had an iron horseshoe cruelly fastened to each of her hands and the soles of her feet.

To say the least, McKinnon was very shocked to discover that hearts are not so faithful, and friends are not so true. To his neighbours he explained that his wife had been practising the black arts behind his back.

Someone said Aonghas left for pastures green and word about him did come back to Skye. It was anything but good.

8. The Devil's Buttermilk

Certain plants have long been associated with the Devil. Best known among them is the stinging nettle, the bane of bare-legged children. Another is the elder tree, whose pithy timber is of no use for carpentry or even as firewood. Mind you, it is interesting to note that people found ways to make wine from both nettles and the flowers and fruit of the elder. These two plants grow happily together. They were always to be found in and around human dwellings and grew best in shady undis-turbed corners where people dumped the cinders and ash from their fires. Perhaps their liking for these conditions is the origin of their association with the fires of Hell and the Devil.

I came across this tale in Swire's The Inner Hebrides and their Legends. *She ascribes it to the Isle of Skye, but it could have originated anywhere. Given the part played by St Columba, Iona might lay equal claim to it. I have stayed relatively faithful to Swire's version with the addition of just a few highlights and some dialogue.*

It was always a great source of annoyance to the Devil that he should be associated with such seemingly useless and unloved plants as the nettle and the elder. He longed for something from the plant realm more befitting his position as the Prince of Darkness. And so, in despair, he appealed to Colm Cille (St Columba), the kind-hearted Irish missionary priest beloved of both Gael and Pict, who founded the monastery on Iona from which he spread Christianity throughout the Kingdom of Dál Riada and beyond.

Well, always the peacemaker, Colm Cille prayed to God, asking if the Devil might be allowed a more auspicious tree or a bush or even a flower. God was touched by Colm Cille's compassion and, after some considerable thought, decided that he could spare a little and hitherto unknown grass called barley, with which the Devil could surely do no harm. The Devil was to spread the plant and let mankind make of it what he would. When Colm Cille told the Devil of God's favour-able decree, the Prince of Darkness was over the moon and went away feeling very pleased with the honour that had been bestowed on him.

Along the road to Vaternish he met Wolf, an old and loyal servant.

'Good day Wolf,' said Oul Nick. 'What devilment has you out and about this evening?' Well, Wolf was taken aback by his master's unusually cheerful mood.

'Good day, oh darkest one,' said Wolf as he bowed down to show his respect. 'May I be so bold as to enquire why your royal darkness is in such a bright and breezy mood?'

'This very day,' said the Devil, 'God has seen fit to bestow on me the honour of a very special plant which better becomes my standing in the world.'

'Oh that is wonderful news, your royal darkness, just absolutely the best news I have heard this day. In fact, your royal darkness …'

'Oh shut up Wolf, you're getting on my nerves.'

'I'm so sorry, your royal darkness. I beg your forgiveness, may I be so bold as to enquire … I mean I just wondered, this plant of which you speak … does it have a name?'

Well, a whole day had passed since Colm Cille had told the Devil about his plant. In the meantime, the Devil had fantasized wildly about how this special plant would increase his powers of darkness as he spread it around the world. Not being particularly interested in the fine detail of things, the name of the plant had slipped out of his mind.

'Hell's gates, what is the name of that damnation plant again?' he roared, but the more he tried to think of it the more his mind became blank and the more infuriated he became.

Sensing he was about to get the blame and incur the Devil's wrath, Wolf tried to help. Frantically he looked about for inspiration.

'Was it heather, your royal darkness?' asked Wolf hopefully.

'No. Don't be stupid. I would have remembered if it was a plant as common and vulgar as heather.'

'What about rushes then? Was it rushes?'

'Why am I cursed with such a dim-witted servant as you, Wolf? Rushes are a sacred plant to the Christians, you dribbling dog.'

Casting about in desperation now Wolf said, 'What about thistles? Was it the thistle, your royal darkness?'

'Thistles! Hmmm Maybe,' said the Devil as he played around with the word a little more. 'Thistles. Thistles. That sounds familiar. Yes, that is it. I believe I have it. It was thistles. Yes! I am right!' he cried.

'Oh well done your royal darkness. Congratulations,' said Wolf, and he quickly sloped off into the coming night before the Devil noticed he was gone.

Ever since that time the Devil has been busy spreading prickly thistles all over the countryside and making work for poor farmers. But, of course, this is not the end of the story. You see, the will of God cannot be undone by man nor beast, nor even the Devil. That inoffensive little grass God called barley is still, after all, the plant he gave to the Prince of Darkness. And, of course, we all know the use to which barley has most famously been put by man – the making of whisky!

Nowadays most people have forgotten about *whisky*'s long association with Oul Nick, and especially those who like a drop, but the good living folk of Dál Riada never have. From the blue hills of Antrim to the misty Isle of Skye, some people still refer to whisky as The Devil's Buttermilk.

9. The Makers of Dreams

The old woman and man in this mysterious and beautiful story are very fascinating characters indeed. Are they faerie folk or some other ancient otherworldly beings? We are left to ponder, but the old woman puts me in mind of some Cailleach-like spirit made flesh. She and her male companion appear more ancient than the mountain cave they inhabit. They have not only the power to commune with and command animals to do their bidding, but the ability to influence the dreams and doings of humans.

I first came across this story in Swire's The Inner Hebrides and their Legends *and have been fascinated by it ever since. I have fleshed it out a little to my taste but have remained relatively faithful to Swire's version.*

It happened a long time ago on the misty Isle of Skye that a group of young maidens went off up on to the slopes of the Cuillin Hills to collect blaeberries. Far and wide they roamed through the heather in search of the fruit. One of them wandered further up into the hills than she intended, filling her basket with the biggest, juiciest berries. Her name was Caoimhe, and it matched her air and appearance perfectly for it means gentle and beautiful in the native Gaelic tongue.

As she worked, Caoimhe sang the ancient songs her mother had taught her, but then suddenly she noticed that the air had grown cold and damp, and she shivered. 'Someone must have walked over my grave,' she said to herself out of long habit. When she lifted her head, the whole hillside was shrouded in thick sea mist. She called out to her friends but the sound of their laughter and singing had long faded away.

Caoimhe thought if only she kept heading downhill surely she would come to her homestead along the shore, eventually. But her progress was slow and soon evening began to come on. As she felt her way through the heather, she came upon bare rocks and realised that she was in mortal danger of falling over a crag or slipping into a deep gully cut by a burn in the peat. She was hopelessly lost, and no one was going to come looking for her, not through the thick mist and growing darkness.

Suddenly, she heard what sounded like footsteps coming from behind her. They had come to look for her after all. She began to call out.

'I'm here. I'm here. Over here.'

No answer came. Then huge, ghostly figures with arms raised as if in anger loomed towards her through the murk. Caoimhe was terrified. She wanted to run, but she stood her ground – more out of fear than courage. The figures came closer and closer and when they were but a few feet away she saw that it was only a herd of red deer and that the raised arms were just the antlers of the stags.

The deer were not in the least bit afraid of Caoimhe. Even so, they soon moved off. Although her heart was beating like a drum with fright, Caoimhe decided to trust to their sure-footedness and follow them in the hope that they might lead her onto familiar ground.

Eventually the deer brought her to a cave in a crag on the side of a hill. Caoimhe feared there might be wolves lurking there, but then she realised the deer would have sensed the danger. She peered into the mouth of the cave, and to her amazement saw an old man and an old woman, sitting on low stools staring down into a pool of crystal-clear water.

Caoimhe cleared her throat, and when the old woman looked up from the pool and saw the deer, she lifted her stool and a pail and came out to milk the hinds.

'What brings you here?' she said over her shoulder to Caoimhe as she worked.

'I was lost and the deer led me to you. Can you give me food and shelter please, just for the night?'

'No, my dear. That we cannot do,' she said. 'But for a year and one night you may stay with us, and that only if you help with the milking of the hinds and the cheese-making.'

Caoimhe looked out into the swirling mist. Darkness was falling fast. What could she do? There was no option but agree to the old woman's terms.

The next day Caoimhe set to work milking the hinds as the old woman showed her. She gathered wild herbs – golden spikes of bog asphodel and fragrant bog myrtle. She found mountain thyme on the high slopes and water mint down by the burns. She learned how to dry these herbs and sprinkle them on the fire over which the sour milk was heated and turned into curds. From these was drained the whey and the soft crowdie cheese was made. All this the old woman patiently taught Caoimhe to do.

Every day the old woman and the old man gazed into the pool in which, the old man said, they could see a reflection of the whole world. Caoimhe made far more cheese than ever they could eat but it did not go to waste. The old man used the cheese to made likenesses of the things and the people he saw in the pool. In the evenings, he took them outside and held them up to the setting sun.

'These in my right hand are the sweet dreams of the innocent,' he said. 'They will all come true.'

At that he invoked the spirits of the eagle and the falcon and the skylark to come down from the heavens and take the good dreams out into the world.

'In my left hand are the wasteful visions of the wicked. They will all prove false.'

And he bid the spirits of the raven and the hoodie crow and the kite to leave off their gory work at carrion and take the evil dreams out into the world.

And so, for a year and a day, Caoimhe worked with the old couple who, in time, she came to understand were the makers of dreams.

'You have proved a good and faithful servant,' said the old woman one morning. 'You must leave now with our blessing. Look for the sign of the moon; your reward awaits you.'

With that, the old woman summoned the deer and they led Caoimhe down the slopes and out of the mist to a shoreline she did not recognise.

Approaching from the sea was a longboat, and Caoimhe felt inclined to run for her life, but the hinds crowded around her for protection. From its prow a fair-haired young man, as handsome a youth as ever she had seen, hailed her. About his neck was a gold pendant in the shape of a crescent moon, and Caoimhe remembered the old woman's words, 'Look for the sign of the moon'.

The young man jumped into the surf and ran ashore. When he reached Caoimhe he dropped to his knees before her.

'You are the woman in my dream,' he said. 'I have searched for you for a year and a day and at last I have found you. I beg you to become my wife and I swear I will be devoted to you for the rest of my days.'

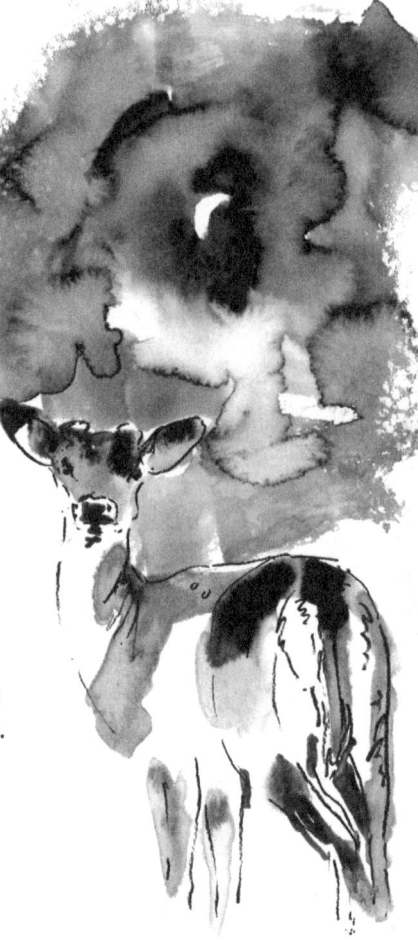

To cut a long story short, Caoimhe, wise girl that she was, agreed, and they sailed across the sea to another island kingdom. Caoimhe's young suitor was the son of a great warrior chieftain. When he brought his wife-to-be home to meet his father and mother there was great feasting and celebrations, and the young couple were joined in marriage.

They had many children, and in time Caoimhe became the queen of her husband's clan and she was well loved. She taught her people how to make the crowdie cheese from the hinds' milk. She brought joy to their dreams and soothed their nightmares. She shared her wise council throughout the land, and while she and her husband reigned, peace and harmony and justice prevailed. But, as I have said, this was all a great many years ago and sadly much has been forgotten and lost.

10. The Fishermen, the Woman and the Whale

This story of revenge and comeuppance was found is Swire's Skye, The Island and its Legends. *It is a rather unusual take on the shape-shifting witch-type character, who more commonly turns herself into a hare.*

Swire thinks the story strange because the animals witches usually took the form of were not eaten by people (the example she gives is the hare). In the north of Ireland, and perhaps it was the same on Skye, some people are said to have turned their noses up at the idea of eating hares. Apparently this may have been because a skinned hare is human-like in appearance, and it squeals like a child when threatened or in pain. Whales, of course, did form a part of the diet of coastal communities – certainly in the mid-seventeenth century. Swire postulates that this supposed anomaly points to the possibility that the story is very much older. It may well be, but Swire's rationale is debatable.

Since time began, young boys have been mischievous and – on occasions, when their parents are less watchful and caring than they should be – the bane of their neighbours. So it was at a place called Uig on the shores of Loch Snizort on the Isle of Skye one time. There, three young friends, cousins and close neighbours most likely, ran wild. Their fathers were often at sea fishing or mending nets, and the mothers, burdened with household chores and many other snotty-nosed and hungry children, did not keep the close eye to their errant sons that they might have.

Nearby there lived an old woman who was strange in her ways. Most folk let her keep herself to herself, but not the three young boys. Egged on by stories they had heard from the mouths of adults about the old woman being some class of a witch, and their own boyish devilment, they often played tricks on her. They put sods over her lum (chimney) and filled her cabin with reek. They stole her peats and put rotten eggs under her hens. They threw stones and called her unspeakable names until the poor woman was near demented. When she went to their parents to complain she got little change, so she cursed them:

'Oh may ye never prosper and may ye never thrive. May all your labours be in vain, as long as you're alive.'

Time passed and the boys grew up. They forgot about the old woman and her curse. Eventually the boys grew into young men as the last carefree days of youth faded away. Always being so close, they decided to throw in their lots together. They built their own currach and knit their own nets.

Despite the best of preparations, they were the most unfortunate and hapless fishermen anyone roundabout could remember. Every day their nets were ripped and torn or lost and their catches so small as to not be worth the bother. The cause of all their trouble and woe was a great whale that had taken up residence in Loch Snizort. They tried everything to scare the whale away, but it seemed determined to stay within the shelter of that sea loch.

One day the fishermen got close enough to thrust a three-pronged pitchfork right into its flank. The whale bucked and with its mighty flukes thrashed the bloody water into a pinkish, white foam before it dived under the waves. The poor creature was never seen again. The next day someone found the old woman lying by the shore nearly dead. She had a row of three deep wounds to her side.

Whether or not the old woman was revived I couldn't tell you, but some people say those three fishermen never had anything but bad luck.

11. The Wise Chieftains

This clever and heartsome little story is, albeit tongue in cheek, an object lesson in feudal diplomacy. As a means of settling clan disputes, however, a not dissimilar system of justice was probably often required if not an everyday essential.

Taken from a version found in Swire's Skye, the Island and its Legends, *this wisdom-type tale is surely one of the best. Sadly, however, wise leaders were and still are few and far between. A later story about the last battle between the MacLeods and the MacDonalds of Skye tells how each side decimated the other, leaving only old men and women to bury their dead!*

For long many a year the MacLeods and the MacDonalds of Skye were at each other's throats. There were periods of relative peace and others of bloody violence. One time, however, the two clan chiefs came together in a spirit of goodwill and agreed to cease all hostilities. In a gesture of friendship, the MacLeod chieftain invited the MacDonald chieftain to Dunvegan Castle, seat of the MacLeods for centuries, and the invitation was graciously accepted.

All was going well but, unknown to the MacLeod, a row was brewing among his clan. A certain clansman grazed his cattle along the cliffs between Forse and Idrigall, as he was quite entitled to do. Another clansman moored his boat in a sheltered cleft in the rocks below the cliffs at Forse as he was quite entitled to do.

Unfortunately, one of the cows slipped and fell over the cliffs. As bad luck would have it, the tide was in and the boat being high up near the shore was directly below. The cow crashed into the boat, smashing it to smithereens, and breaking its neck all at once.

The owner of the cow was fit to be tied, but so too was the owner of the boat.

'If your boat hadn't been there, my cow would have fallen into the water and swam ashore. I demand recompense for my loss,' said the owner of the cow.

'If your heavy-footed beast hadn't fallen on my birlinn it would still be afloat. I demand recompense for my loss,' cried the owner of the boat.

And so, arguments went back and forth, neither being able to see the other's point of view. The row began to drag in other clan members from each side and bloodshed threatened to split the MacLeods. The grievances were brought before the MacLeod chief for his judgement just as he sat down to break bread with the MacDonald. 'No matter who I find for,' he thought to himself, 'the other will be slighted and my clan will splinter nonetheless.'

At last, MacLeod had the idea, wily old fox that he was, that if he asked MacDonald to pass judgement then his clansmen could not accuse him of favouring either side and might accept the decision less grudgingly.

'Would you be kind enough to grace us poor MacLeods with your great wisdom in this matter?' Macleod asked MacDonald, thinking he was playing to the other chieftain's vanity.

'With pleasure,' said MacDonald, realising he was being placed between the Devil and the deep blue sea.

Both clansmen were called and given the chance to put forward his case.

'If his boat hadn't been there my cow would have fallen into the water and swam ashore. I demand recompense for my loss,' said the owner of the cow.

'If his clumsy-footed beast hadn't slipped and fallen, my bir-linn would still be afloat. I demand recompense for my loss,' cried the owner of the boat.

'Hmm,' said the MacDonald chief and he closed his eyes in contemplation for a long time. Some thought he had fallen asleep, but eventually he lifted his brow and opened his eyes.

'Who owns this cliff at Forse?' he asked.

'I do,' declared the MacLeod without hesitation.

'I see,' said MacDonald thoughtfully, 'Well, if the cow had not fallen from the *cliff* the boat would not have been dam-aged. And if the boat had not been moored under the shelter of the *cliff* the cow would not have been killed. Therefore, the fault lies with the owner of the *cliff*, and he alone should pay compensation to both the owner of the cow and the boat.'

There was a loud cheer, and although the MacDonald chief-tain had found against his host, the MacLeod chieftain was heartily glad, for MacDonald's judgement seemed to please everyone. Indeed, all there agreed that both the MacLeod and his guest the MacDonald were both very wise chieftains and worthy of their clan's fealty.

12. The Child of Swan Bay

It is hard to imagine a more beautiful and moving swan story than the 'Children of Lir', but this folk tale with its much happier ending surely comes very close. Yet again, it comes from Swire's The Inner Hebrides and their Legends, *which has proved to be such a treasure trove of spellbinding tales.*

The classic scenario of the cruel stepmother is widespread in European folklore, but this adaptation set in the splendid scenery of north-east Skye must be among one of the most enchanting.

Near Staffin Bay on the beautiful north-east coast of Skye is a place known to the locals as Swan Bay. Since time out of memory wild white swans have come here every winter for sanctuary and respite from colder climes further north.

Long years past, no one now remembers how long ago it was, a little girl lived along the shore here. Her father had been called upon by his chieftain and was away fighting in some local war or skirmish, she knew not where. Her mother being long dead, the girl's father had taken another wife and, as is so often the case, the stepmother was anything but good to the child. In her father's absence, his new wife, hard-hearted woman that she was, turned his daughter out of her childhood home to fend for herself.

Cold and frightened, the child turned to the sea as so many lost souls do. While she sat there shivering by the shore with nothing but a thin woollen shawl to keep out the cold, the swans slowly approached. They were curious and the child did not shy away.

Before the little girl knew it, she was surrounded by huge white wings. She felt the warmth and softness of their downy under-feathers, and hard beaks gently preened the tats in her tousled hair.

More swans came and gathered around. Each began to pluck feathers from its back or breast or wings or tail. They wove the feathers into the child's shawl and soon she bore a cape of soft, warm, snow-white feathers. And so, the little girl stayed with the swans. She rode on their backs as they paddled from place to place and, to her sheer delight, they even took her on short flights across the bay. Two years she lived as a swan, and in spring when the birds flew north they took her with them.

Much to the stepmother's surprise, for she thought her husband long dead and had taken up with another man, he returned home after two long years of campaigning.

'Where is my child?' was the first thing he asked.

'She is dead two winters past,' came the sharp rely. 'As I thought you were, my husband.'

'I am not your husband any longer,' the man growled. 'Tell me you buried my daughter with her mother,' he roared at her.

There were more lies and weasel words but, as always, the truth appeared in the end. Neighbours bore witness against the woman and the chieftain declared that all who had cheated or betrayed his warriors while they were in the service of the clan would be punished.

The next night, the poor, war-weary, grieving man went down to the shore, for like his daughter he was drawn there in his despair. Through the soft evening light came the steady whirr of wings. It was the swans returned. Hundreds of them came into land with a swishing and hissing of water and a haunting chorus of whooping voices. Even in his grief the man was in awe at the sight of so many of the great white birds.

Among them near the shore he suddenly spied a child. He would hardly have recognised his daughter, so grown and elegant had she become, but she had the unmistakable and lovely looks of her mother. There was great joy in the man's cabin that night and in his chieftain's household, for all who had mourned the loss of such an innocent child now rejoiced at her wondrous return.

As for the child, she seemed bewildered, for she had lost the power of speech and had developed some strange bird-like habits. Though her human voice came back to her, for years after she liked nothing better than to bathe, summer or winter, where a stream ran down from the mountain into the sea. She was inclined, also, to stand on one leg, ankle deep in water with her head resting on her shoulder staring out to sea for hours on end.

She never forgot her swan family and neither did the folk of her clan. Every year they greeted the swans. All through the freezing winter days, when the waves broke in curling sugary sea ice, they carried food down to the shore. Swan Bay became a sanctuary for those birds and all their descendants.

RAASAY

13. The Witches' Revenge

Found in Sir George Douglas' Scottish Fairy and Folk Tales
(A.L. Burt Company, New York, 1901) this story is set around the
same period as when King James VI of Scotland believed that witches
intent on his death tried to sink his ship. This was in 1589, and the
investigation into these events led to the North Berwick Witch Trials
of 1590, resulting in the arrest, torture and death of a great many.
King James subsequently wrote Daemonologie, *a book in condemna-*
tion of witchcraft published in 1597. Against such a backdrop, this story
is all the more remarkable insofar as the witch characters triumph over
their tormentor.

   It is interesting and shocking to note that in a period of just over two
hundred years ending in about 1707, between 3,000 and 4,000 accused
women are thought to have been put to death as witches. Outrageous as
this statistic is, it does not begin to expose the brutality and fear visited
on women during this time.

   I have developed the role of the old woman by placing her onboard the
vessel and suggesting the plague of cats comes directly from her. This, I
hope, makes the narrative flow a little better.

It was many long centuries ago that a bloodline of the MacLeods
of Lewis also became the lairds of Raasay – the larger of the
small islands off the eastern shore of Skye. In due course, John
Garve MacGillichallum (son of Malcolm) inherited the title of
Raasay, and in his time he was hailed as a fearless warrior and

generous clan chieftain. But not every inhabitant of that isle was so favourably disposed towards their laird.

The Raasay was committed to seeking out all members of a sisterhood of hags he suspected of practising the dark arts. At that time, he supposed there to be a great many such women dwelling on Raasay and the islets roundabout. MacGillichallum and his followers took great delight in driving them into the sea or otherwise bringing about their demise.

To cut a long story short, it happened that the Raasay and a few of his closest friends were intent on a stag-hunting trip to his ancestral lands on the isle of Lewis, famous for the quantity and quality of its deer. They all set out of a fine morning aboard the laird's birlinn, bound for the north of Lewis across the Minch. After the short crossing the men and their hounds landed, and a fine day of hunting was had by all. Many harts and hinds were taken down, and to celebrate their successes an evening of feasting and ceilidhing soon followed.

The next morning the company arose with the dawn, intending to return to Raasay to share out the venison among family and friends, and perhaps continue their revelry. The sea, however, had turned treacherous. Great westerly squalls swept across the Minch, whipping up white horses and warning of a perilous crossing. Some among the party urged the Raasay to wait until the weather settled, but he was not a man to back away from adventure and his courage knew no bounds.

To rally his men, the Raasay brought them to the Ferry House on Lewis, where they partook of something to revive their flagging mettle – *uisge beatha* – the water of life! As the whiskey went down, their spirits soared. Voices rose and arguments mounted about the wisdom of attempting a crossing of the Minch in such weather. Just as MacGillichallum was holding forth and making one last plea to convince his men that all would be well, an old woman entered the tavern. She was dressed in rags and supported herself on a twisted branch for a crutch. Her skin was more wrinkled than the bark of an oak and she had not a single tooth in her head, but her dark green eyes were as sharp as a bird's.

'Good morning grandmother,' said the Raasay, silencing all with his reverential tone.

'Good morning to you sir,' said she in return.

'May I beg forgiveness for my unruly friends, whose fear has been aroused by a little wind and weather. What crumb of wisdom or comfort might you have to offer them?'

'Far be it from me to counsel such worldly gentlemen – and though I am nearer the grave than any of ye, still I hold dear to my life. I would have no fear on the sea today and if ye'll take me with ye back to Raasay I would gladly pay my way.'

'Not a ha'penny will you pay, grandmother. You will come aboard as my guest, for you have shown these faint-hearted fools what true courage is.'

With that, tumblers were raised and there was a loud cheer. The Raasay ordered his crew to prepare the birlinn for the crossing and the whole party went aboard the little vessel.

They soon set sail for Raasay, but no sooner had they left the shelter of their berth than the wind picked up a notch and the waves seemed certain to overwhelm them. Attempts were made to put about and return to Lewis, but the sea conditions forbade it. The elements conspired to push the birlinn further and further out into the Minch, where she was tossed about like a leaf. Only the chieftain and the old woman seemed undaunted. Everyone else onboard was in great fear of their lives.

The Raasay tried to uplift the hearts of his men by calling attention to the fearlessness displayed by their passenger as an example, but they kept their heads bowed. He took the helm himself and steered a course through the tempest down towards the east coast of Skye and some blessed sanctuary. His show of courage inspired all. Soon the storm felt as though it might be falling and the dread that had gripped everyone began to lift. As they neared the island of Raasay, the chieftain's eye was taken by a strange sight up near the top of the mast. It was a huge black cat, glaring back down at him with fierce green eyes. He searched the vessel and could see no sign of the old woman. Only her twisted crutch lay where she had been seated near the bow a few moments before.

The Raasay hurled a curse at the feline and ordered his men to climb into the rigging and dislodge the creature. As the words left his mouth, the she-cat gave birth to a litter of little clones that seemed to multiply and grow with every second that went by. In a very short time, every rope and spar was covered with black cats. Within sight and hailing distance of their journey's end, the number of cats became so great that their weight made the birlinn top-heavy and she toppled over. All onboard were pitched into the swirling waters and soon disappeared beneath the waves.

The birlinn was found wrecked along the shore the following day, but the plague of cats was nowhere to be found. Not a single man survived, and that was the way in which John Garve MacGillichallum, Laird of Raasay, met his end. It was often told on the island of Raasay and the islets roundabout that the women he had so mercilessly persecuted had summoned all their kith and kin and all their powers to take cold revenge.

EIGG

14. The Inquisitive Ghost

Eigg is one of the 'small islands' of the Inner Hebrides between Skye and Mull. It has been inhabited since earliest times, as evidence of Neolithic activity shows. The island also boasts Iron and Bronze Age sites. An old legend says that remarkably large and powerful women resided in a dun by the shores of Loch nam Ban Móra and Eigg was once known as Eilean nam Ban Móra – The Island of the Great Women. Whether the ghostly woman in this story is one of the Ban Móra, I cannot say, but she is certainly very forceful.

Like a lot of old folk tales subsumed by the influence of Christianity, a favourable outcome is often brought about a clergyman or saint. In this case, the otherworldly spirit is eventually undone by the power of the 'Good Book' – the Bible.

This little sketch has been developed from the version found in McGregor's The Peat Fire Flame.

It was once said that an old, wizened ghost of a witch or faerie woman haunted a certain place on the Isle of Eigg. At ungodly hours she appeared to islanders travelling along what was grandly called the King's Highway, but which was, in truth, the only road on the island and little more than a rutted single track.

Late one night the son of a local crofter had cause to be abroad alone. He was going to a neighbouring croft on an errand for his father. The lad was not well known for the sharpness of his mind, but he was a harmless being.

Sure enough, as he made his way along the road, didn't he come across the old carlin. She was hideous. Her face was wrinkled like the skin of a fish kept too long in the salt and her filthy grey hair hung down in long wispy strands from under her hood.

As the lad approached, she opened her toothless, gaping mouth.

'From where have ye come?' she demanded in a screeching voice that would have convinced any mortal man with the slightest hint of wit to run for his life.

'From my father's house,' answered the lad innocently.

'And where is your father's house?'

'Where my grandfather built it.'

'And where did your grandfather build it?'

'Where my father lives now.'

'But where does your father live?'

'In the house I've just come from.'

'And where have you just come from?' screamed the old woman.

'From me father's house!' answered the lad.

'But where in all creation is your father's house?'

'Didn't I just tell ye before?' said the lad, riled up now. 'Where my grandfather built it!'

And so it went back and forth until the first grey light of dawn appeared, at which time the old woman vanished into the mist and the lad went on his weary way.

'Where the hell were you to this time?' his father cried when he eventually came home.

When the lad explained what had happened, his father vowed to settle the old woman's hash once and for all. The next evening, he armed himself with a Bible and went to the place where his son said he had beheld the apparition. When the old wraith appeared and began to ask him the same impertinent questions, he blessed himself and shook the holy book in her face. Without another word, she vanished into the night.

The old people always said that it took Gaoth a Bhiohaill, the Wind of the Bible, to drive the ghost of the old woman away from Isle of Eigg. Where she went nobody knows, but some say she will return one day when the good folk of Eigg are least prepared.

MUCK

15. The Death of Diarmuid

In this excerpt from the famous Irish story 'The Pursuit of Diarmuid and Gráinne', the traditional setting for the climax shifts from Benbulben Mountain in Sligo to the Isle of Muck in the Hebrides. In other versions the boar they are hunting is called the Great Boar of Caledon – not to be confused with the Calydonian Boar of Greek mythology. As with other tales from the Fenian Cycle, variants exist both in Ireland and Scotland, giving endless scope for tongue-in-cheek debate between Irish and Scottish storytellers.

I have developed this unusual version mainly from that found in Swire's The Inner Hebrides and their Legends.

As everyone knows, Fionn mac Cumhaill was the strongest and wisest and most famed leader of a band of heroic warrior poets known as the Fianna. They had taken an oath that bound them to protect Erin from all her enemies. But godlike as they were, they still retained some mortal failings.

After the death of Fionn mac Cumhaill's wife Maigneis, the great man was bereft. To ease their leader's grief, Fionn's men arranged a marriage with Gráinne, the young daughter of the High King of Ireland, Cormac mac Airt. The young princess, who had little or no say in the matter, was not overjoyed by the idea of marrying the now-aging Fionn mac Cumhaill, notwithstanding his grand reputation.

At the betrothal feast Gráinne met the young and handsome hero Diarmuid. He bore on his forehead a magical love spot that made him irresistible to any and all women who laid eyes upon it. Diarmuid tried to shield women from this power, but during the feast he became careless and, sure enough, when Gráinne saw it she fell helplessly in love with him.

In the throes of her passion, she slipped a sleeping draft into the mead and ale and soon afterwards all the revellers fell fast asleep – all except Diarmuid.

'I beg you,' she said to Diarmuid, 'carry me away from here this very night and I will be your true love forever.'

'Gráinne, you are the most beautiful and desirable woman I have ever seen, but I cannot marry you. I will not betray Fionn mac Cumhaill and my comrades of the Fianna.'

Many more hot-blooded words passed between them, and slowly Gráinne's considerable feminine wiles and charms began to weaken Diarmuid's strength of will. Eventually, Gráinne got her way, and the lovers fled.

To shorten a long story, the lovers were hunted all over Erin and many adventures and narrow escapes did they have. But Diarmuid still had many friends within the ranks of the Fianna, including the likes of Oscar, Fionn's own grandson. With their help and interventions, a bloody end to this sorry affair was avoided. Fionn and Diarmuid were eventually reconciled and Diarmuid was allowed to live in peace with Gráinne.

Stories about what happened next have been told the length and breadth of Erin for many centuries. Depending on the teller, settings have varied, but the ending is always the same.

On the little Scottish island of Muck in the Hebrides, also known as the Isle of Pigs, it was said that there lived a race of wild boar with venomous bristles. Always keen on the chase, the men of the Fianna often went across the sea to Muck to pit themselves against these most ferocious of swine.

On one hunting trip Diarmuid fatally wounded a huge boar. He went forward to put the creature out of its misery, but with its dying kick it pricked Diarmuid's skin with one of its deadly bristles. Diarmuid fell to the ground as the venom went through him. Seeing his young friend in mortal danger, Fionn ran to the Well of Healing and returned with a mouthful of life-giving water in his cupped hands. As he stood before his dying friend, he remembered how Diarmuid had taken Gráinne, his young wife to be, and in so doing had dishonoured him, and he let the water trickle through his fingers on to the ground.

But then his love for Diarmuid quickly got the better of his pride. He ran back to the Well of Healing a second time and returned with another mouthful of the water in his big hands. But the old resentment and anger rose up in him and he wrestled with his still hurt pride. Slowly he let the water trickle on to the ground once more.

But then he felt the sting of shame and remorse, and so for the third time Fionn ran to the Well of Healing. He returned with more of the life-giving water. This time he went straight to Diarmuid. He knelt by his side and tried to moisten his comrade's lips. Alas, it was too late. The water trickled down Diarmuid's chin into his beard and he breathed his last in Fionn's arms.

And so, the strongest and the wisest leader of the Fianna, the most famed warrior of them all, Fionn mac Cumhaill, proved that he too could be as weak as any man. It is said that though he never shed a tear in his whole life, Fionn hung his head in shame and felt the pain of grief for the loss of his friend.

ARDNAMURCHAN

16. Luran and the Charmed Knowe

Ardnamurchan is the name given to a remote and unspoiled peninsula jutting out into the Atlantic Ocean between the isles of Skye and Mull. At its furthest extent is the most westerly point of mainland Britain, on which sits a lighthouse.

Adomnán, also known as Eunan, who was the Abbot of Iona c.679–704, suggests that the place was settled by Irish Gaels in his time. Presumably they brought their stories and their faeries with them!

Like many other stories, this classic scenario of faerie lore is to be found from the Isle of Skye to the Antrim Glens, and further afield. I have developed this version, with a dark twist or two in the tail, from two accounts found in McGregor's book The Peat Fire Flame *and* John Gregorson Campbell's Superstitions of the Highlands and Islands of Scotland *(James MacLehose and Sons, Glasgow, 1900).*

Just above the southern shore of the Ardnamurchan headland is a wee hill known locally as the Charmed Knowe. It was once said to be inhabited by faerie folk, and might be yet for all I know. At the foot of this hill, many years ago, there lived a farmer by the name of Luran or the Son of the Dark Man. Luran kept a small herd of cattle that were his wealth and only means of keeping body and soul together.

One morning Luran found that one of his cows had died during the night. He was greatly vexed for she had been fit and well the evening before. As he looked over the animal's carcass, he found a sewing needle sticking out from its shoulder. Worse was to come. The next morning Luran found another of his cows dead. Again, he found a needle sticking out from its shoulder, and so it followed every morning for a week until Luran was beside himself with grief and woe.

Not knowing what on Earth could be causing the sudden mysterious deaths of his treasured animals, but fearing some evil or otherworldly hand, Luran decided to keep a watch. On the very next night a culvert in the side of the Charmed Knowe opened. A band of faerie folk stole out into the darkness and set about herding one of Luran's cows back into the hillside. When Luran saw this, he joined in the herding and followed the faerie folk into their own domain to see what they were doing.

He could hardly believe his eyes when the wee folk duly cut the poor animal's throat and began to skin it. No sooner had the faeries robbed the cow of its hide but they stuffed it with dry grass and began to sew it back up again. They placed one of their own within and the pelt was then neatly sewn up from inside.

No human mind can understand the workings and weavings of the faerie folk and Luran was, not surprisingly, at a loss. Even so, when he saw his tormentors begin to roll the mannequin of his cow down the hill into the field he joined in. This strange act of wantonness seemed to prompt great joviality and merriment, and the faeries began playing music and drinking and dancing and feasting. Luran joined in the dancing but was sure not to touch a morsel of the faerie food or a drop of their liquor. He knew that to do so would make him a prisoner of the Otherworld forever.

As the night wore on, one by one the faeries lay down to sleep, and eventually only Luran was still awake. It was then he chose to help himself to a faerie goblet – 'To make up for my losses,' he said to himself. There were countless glittering cups standing on the tabletops. 'Surely,' thought Luran, 'they will not miss one.' With a deep breath he made his move and edged towards the still-open culvert with the goblet under his coat. But the moment Luran stepped outside the Charmed Knowe the faeries stirred. Up went cries of, 'Thief! Thief!', and curses the likes of which Luran had never heard before were hurled after him as he ran down the hill for his life.

It was then Luran realised the folly of his actions, for he knew he could not outrun the faerie folk and would surely pay for his crime against them. A stitch came into his side and his lungs heaved in his breast. Just as he felt the faeries were about to snatch his coattails did he hear a voice hailing him from somewhere in the darkness.

'Luran, Son of the Dark Man, get thee among the black stones down by the shore.'

With every ounce of strength left in him, Luran made for the shore and the rocks still wet and slippery from the ebbing tide. It was then he remembered that no faerie could venture beyond the line reached by the highest tide. As Luran shivered among the rocks, he heard the cries of some mortal man in great distress, as if being beaten by a throng. He believed this to be the poor soul who had guided him towards the shore, though never did he discover the true identity of this person.

After dawn Luran, shivering from the cold and hunger, made for home. On his way he found his dead cow at the bottom of the hill where he had helped the faeries roll it the night before. From its shoulder was sticking out a needle.

Some say Luran sold the cup for a tidy sum of money, but if he did he never seemed to prosper much for his dealings. Others say that he was spellbound by the cup and could never part with it.

Years later, as he was sailing across to Inverary, his boat was beset by a sudden squall and sank. Luran, Son of the Dark

Man, was lost and presumed drowned. It was often whispered, though, that he was taken by a faerie wind. What became of him no one could swear to, for his body was never found. Whatever the case may be, that was the last anyone ever heard mention of Luran or the faerie cup.

All I can tell you for certain is that no human mind can understand the workings and weavings of the faerie folk. They are best left to their own devices, for they never forget or forgive a slight against them.

LISMORE

17. Beothail's Bones

Throughout Dál Riada there are tales of Norse princesses buried in cer-
tain places for various reasons. According to Alisdair Alpin McGregor,
for example, one was said to be buried under a cairn high up on the
slopes of Beinn na Caillich, near Broadford on Skye so that for the rest
of eternity she might 'lie in the wake of the winds from Norway'.

Another called Biornal, the sister of Storab, a Norse prince murdered
by the people of Raasay, requested to be buried on top of a mountain
known as Sron Bhiornal (Sron Vourlinn) on Skye. From here she
could overlook the accursed island where her beloved brother was slain
and which, in revenge, she was said to have 'harried with fire and
sword'. And there are other stories of 'big women' or 'goddess queens'
of Viking origin buried on Islay, Jura and other places.

The following story, however, is surely one of the most interest-
ing and unusual of this type. This rendering has been reworked from
various sources, but the bones, if you'll forgive the pun, I found in
McGregor's The Peat Fire Flame.

The island of Lismore lies in the mouth of Loch Linnhe
between the Lynn of Lorne and the Lynn of Morven, north-
east of Mull. In ancient times it was known as the Great
Garden, so fertile was its soil.

On Lismore centuries ago there lived a merciless Viking
prince called Caifen, after which Castle Coeffin was named.
The castle was built years later on the site of Caifen's

stronghold on the north-west coast of the island. Caifen's reputation as a fearsome warrior was well earned. It was said he always kept his longships ready for battle and neither allowed his men to rest nor their swords to rust.

With Caifen lived his sister, the beautiful Beothail. She was said to be as fair and gentle as her brother was dark and fierce. But Beothail had a lover, and he was as dauntless as any of his Viking kinfolk. For his daring and lust for battle, however, he paid with his life. When the news that he had been slain on some distant shore reached Beothail, she fell down ill with grief. Slowly she grew wan and weak and eventually died for the loss of her love.

Amid great sadness, Beothail was buried on a knoll close to her brother's fortress. Not long after, though, her spirit awoke from its death-sleep. Beothail began to appear to Caifen and to others, always weeping and wailing and tearing her hair. Night after night Beothail's ghost was seen and heard begging her brother, 'Take me back to the land of my birth and bury me among my ancestors.'

The pleas of Beothail's restless spirit even reached her father's ears and, mourning the loss of his beloved daughter, the old Viking king sent a longship with orders that she was to be unearthed.

'All traces of the foreign soil are to be washed from her bones before she is brought back home for reburial.'

His instructions were carried out to the letter and Beothail's decaying corpse was taken up. Her remains were bathed in a local holy well that was blessed by St Moluag, the patron saint of Lismore and a disciple of the great St Columba.

With great ceremony, her earthly remains were wrapped in a fresh shroud. She was borne away northwards over the sea to be buried once again. But even on the voyage home her spirit could not be pacified. All through the long nights she wept and wailed ceaselessly and not a man aboard that longship could take his sleep undisturbed. When at last she was lain down among the dust and mouldering remains of her ancestors, still her ghost would not rest.

Once again she was exhumed and her corpse closely examined by the Viking holy men and wise women. Only then did one woman notice that the bones of one of her toes were missing. Immediately her father dispatched another longship to the isle of Lismore. When St Moluag's Well was searched the little bones were found, washed clean and white, in the gravel at the bottom. Not until these last fragments of Beothail's body were placed in the ground along with the rest of her earthly remains did the Viking princess find eternal peace.

And that's the story of Beothail, the Viking princess who was buried not once but three times. To this day the place where she was first buried and disentombed appears as an empty grave, but mercifully it is still and quiet.

MULL

18. The Wise Mother

Wise women were those females who were once possessed of such knowledge as country folk depended upon for everything from infertility to childbirth. They were herbalists and holders of recipes and charms and cures for all manner of maladies from toothache to smallpox, and a lot more besides. Volumes could be written on the knowledge that has been lost since these women were replaced by modern medicine.

The following focuses on one aspect of this and features the little carnivorous bog plant commonly known in Gaelic as mòthan *or in English as butterwort (*Pinguicula vulgaris*). It was used as an agent to thicken or curdle milk for cheese-making, but the plant had more magical powers too. It was rubbed on a cow's udder to protect it from someone putting the blink on its production of milk. Milk or cheese made from a cow fed* mòthan *protected the consumer from all interference by the faerie folk. A sprig of it carried by man or woman protected them in the same way, but also against fire and drowning. If someone made a miraculous escape from death, it was said that he or she must have drunk the milk of a cow that ate from the* mòthan.

The outline for this story was also found in McGregor's The Peat Fire Flame.

There was once a shepherd and his wife who dwelt in a lonely bothy in the wilderness near the foot of Ben More on the beautiful Isle of Mull. The wife was a wise woman, and people came to her from round and about for all kinds of concoctions and cures. Often it was she who was summoned in the middle of the night by some neighbour whose poor wife was in the throes of labour. But now the woman was with child herself, and she could feel that something was amiss. She bid her husband to go and fetch the help she would need.

As the shepherd prepared to go out into the night, his wife called him to her bedside.

'Before ye go husband,' she said, 'bring me a bowl of milk and whatever cheese is in the crock. Set it there on a table by the bed.'

Without question the shepherd did as he was asked, and the woman took a sip of the milk and morsel of the cheese.

'Now bring the fire tongs and anything made of iron,' she said.

Again, without a moment's hesitation, the shepherd obeyed.

'Lie the tongs across the foot of bed and that reaping hook there on the windowsill.'

When all was done to her satisfaction, she bid her husband all haste.

'Hurry back now, for my time is near.'

And so it was. The poor woman's labour pains began to come swiftly one after the other as she lay there in that cabin all alone. To cut a long and agonising story short, the child was born before the shepherd returned. Lucky it was that the wee thing survived at all, and its mother was the strong and wise woman that she was.

Not long after her bairn came into this world, the woman suddenly became aware of great malevolence near at hand. The peats on the fire suddenly flared up and the air became chill and rank. In great fear for her child, the woman grasped her bloody newborn and held it up to her breast. Looking around, she thought she could see ghostly shadows moving here and there. Then she heard something that made her own blood turn to ice. It was the voices of unseen faerie women.

'Take the child now and we'll be away,' one callously whispered.

'How can I when she has penned herself and the child in with iron and supped of a cow that has fed on the pearly mòthan?' rasped another angrily.

Just by that the woman's husband burst in the door with the neighbouring midwife, and all danger was forestalled.

'Thank God,' said the woman.

Her husband ran to his wife's bedside and the midwife quickly set about tending to the urgent needs of the child and its mother. Only when the woman and babe had been washed and lay on a bed of fresh linen did the shepherd's wife tell her husband and the midwife the whole story of what had happened in their absence.

'It's a mercy that you are as gifted as you are dearie,' said the shepherd, and mightily relieved he was that his wife was indeed a wise mother.

19. A Sister's Curse

Of excessive pride, jealousy and revenge, this is a very dark story from the Isle of Mull. I have heard of curses issued by widows, priests and saints, but until now never by a sister. This story, in that regard, seems very unusual if not unique.

It was originally published in Lord Archibald Campbell's collection, Waifs and Strays of the Celtic Tradition, *5 Volumes (David Nutt, London, 1889–95), but much more recently appears in* West Highland Tales *by Fitzroy MacLean (William Collins and Company Limited, 1985).*

Regarding the last sheaf tradition, Lord Archibald refers to the Harvest Maiden. It was more commonly referred to as the Harvest

Hare, or Harvest Hag, or in the Gaelic, Cailleach (see Ulster Folklore, *Jeanne Cooper Foster, H.R. Carter Publications Ltd, Belfast, 1951). I have used Harvest Hag to avoid confusion with the character of the Faerie Maiden.*

There was once two grown-up unmarried sisters living together on the south shore of Mull who had been orphaned years before. The local people referred to them as Lovely Margaret and Brown Ailsa. Margaret was tall and slender, and she had long black hair and sapphire-blue eyes. Her skin was as pale and soft as a white rose, and she was indeed lovely. Ailsa was rounder and her hair was mousy. She was, to be blunt about it, very plain.

One day when Lovely Margaret was alone in their cabin, a young handsome stranger came calling. He was tall and fair-haired and had eyes as blue as her own.

'Could you spare a bite of meat and something to drink for a weary and hungry traveller?' he said to Margaret.

'We never turned a stranger away from our door,' she answered, and set him down at the table to a jug of milk and a plate of oatcakes and honey.

The young man ate his meal with great relish, and all the while he held Lovely Margaret in his gaze. When he was finished he took her hands in his and spoke at last.

'You are as beautiful as you are kind,' he said, looking into her eyes.

Well, Margaret was aware of just how beautiful she was, for the neighbour folk were always telling her and she liked to hear their words. Pleased with herself, she went to fetch the stranger more milk but when she returned he was gone without so much as a by-your-leave. A confusion of thoughts raced through her mind at this affront, for one minute he had been as sweet as the honey she poured on his oatcakes, and the next as ill-mannered as a pig. She was angry and disappointed, and at the same time longed to see him again, but when Brown Ailsa came home, all this Margaret kept to herself.

The next day Ailsa was going visiting again to an old aunt as she so often did. Lovely Margaret was not alone long when the fair-haired stranger appeared at the doorway. All feelings of anger and disappointment left her, and she welcomed him in as before. This time, however, the stranger never spoke but took Margaret in his strong arms and kissed her passionately on the lips. It was only afterwards that Margaret thought to herself how readily she had yielded to her lover's charms, for she had never been kissed before. A little embarrassed, the fanciful thought crossed her mind that he had placed her under some kind of a spell.

Over the next few weeks Ailsa went every day to visit their aged relative and Margaret's lover was free to come and go as he pleased. Day after day he called, and sometimes twice. As their romance became deeper and deeper, so did their lovemaking become more and more hot-blooded. When he was with her Maragret was in Heaven, but when they were apart she was in Hell. Night and day she longed for him. The way he talked and the way he carried himself were unlike any man on Mull or the mainland known to her. Often it was that she thought he was not of this world, for he was so completely distinct and unpredictable in his ways.

'You must never mention me or our love to anyone,' he warned her one day, 'or you will never see me again.'

Margaret took his threat seriously but calmly, for by now she would have died for him.

Months passed and one evening Ailsa came home after a few days away. She was bursting to tell her sister some good news.

'I have found a suitor,' she declared. 'His name is Duncan. He is a good man with a dozen cows, a few acres of land and a boy at his command.'

'Well, well sister, you are a dark horse,' said Margaret, quite taken aback.

'He has already given me his word and we are to be married this day month.'

'I will miss you out of the house, sister,' lied Margaret, 'but I wish you both well.'

'Thank you Margaret. I hope someday you will know what love is and find a man who will love you as warmly as my Duncan loves me,' said Ailsa, a little too self-contentedly.

This needled Margaret, for she had always thought of Ailsa as a bit of a prude, and now imagined Duncan as a ruddy-faced bore of a farmer whose only goal in life was to sire a son to take over the wee croft that he scraped a living from.

'And who is to say I haven't already found a bonnie lover?' snapped Lovely Margaret.

'You?' cried Ailsa. 'When? Where?'

'Everyday he comes to me,' boasted Margaret. 'And every day he makes love to me like a wild stallion.'

No sooner had the words left her lips than she regretted her outburst, but it was too late.

'Promise me, sister,' Lovely Margaret begged Ailsa afterwards, 'you won't breathe a word of this to a living soul.'

Ailsa agreed but, of course, she let it slip to her intended, for it was too good a secret to keep. Before much longer it was all over the countryside, and everyone was talking about Lovely Margaret's strange lover. The old folk began to say that they had heard of such things before. That Margaret's lover was no ordinary mortal but was of the *sidhe* – the faerie folk. 'Nothing but sorrow will come of it,' they said.

Weeks went by, and though Margaret kept a watch for her lover, he never returned. Night after night she went to her cold bed wishing he would come, but always she woke up alone. When she went down to the village, everyone stared in a way that told her they knew of her secret. 'If they know,' she fretted to herself, 'then my love will know too, and he will never come back to me, for I have betrayed him.'

Margaret began to neglect herself and the cabin, and it wasn't long after that she took to the roads begging a crust here and byre to lay her head there. Often it was that the folk heard her weeping and wailing how she had betrayed her faerie lover. Margaret felt the terrible pain of guilt and loss, but she also bore nothing but resentment and spite for her sister, who she blamed for all her woes. In her most tormented rants, she called down a curse on her poor sister's head.

> May the grass beneath your feet refuse to grow,
> Nor any crop of grain your man may sew.
> May heat never rise from your fire,
> And your cows drop down dead in the byre
> May your tatties turn to water with the blight.
> And the moths corrupt your meal kist day and night.
> May the faeries take revenge on you for me,
> On the heads of your descendants may it be.

Nine months after Ailsa was married she had a son, and they called him Torquil. Like his father, he was a hard worker, and he grew into a fine, big, strapping man. He became famed throughout the island as a reaper and no man could better him at the harvest time.

One year, Torquil heard about a strange maiden who could reap a field of oats before dawn and far quicker than any man. The folk called her the Faerie Maiden of the Cairn, for some had said they saw her rise out from a jumble of rocks on the hillside. Egged on by this story, the proud young man felt the need to challenge her. Of a Sunday evening, he waited until the sun had set. Sure enough, by the light of the moon he spied a beautiful maiden step into the field and begin to reap. Determined to best her, Torquil started into the reaping beside her, but she was possessed of a great energy and speed. The harder Torquil worked, the farther ahead of him got the maiden.

'Delay, delay, oh Faerie Maiden of the Cairn,' called Torquil.

'Overtake me, overtake me, oh handsome brown-haired youth,' came the reply.

Try as he might, Torquil could not overtake the maiden. All night they worked, and just before dawn the Faerie Maiden of the Cairn stood at the head of the last furrow waiting for Torquil to cut the final sheaf. Eventually he came up towards her, the sweat dripping from his brow and his back breaking for want of a rest.

In those days it was the custom to cut the last sheaf and fashion it into a doll. Known as the Harvest Hag, she was kept for good luck until the following year. The farmers held firmly to their ancient rituals and on no account would anyone have done this deed on a Monday for it was thought that to do so on the Day of the Moon would invite terrible misfortune.

'It is an evil thing you have done,' said the Faerie Maiden of the Cairn, 'to reap the Harvest Hag on this sacred day.'

Only then did Torquil realise that in his efforts to catch the beguiling faerie maiden, he had not realised that Sunday had turned to Monday. It was too late. As the thought passed through his mind, he fell down dead with exhaustion, never to speak another word. Always it was said that through the otherworldly endeavours of the Faerie Maiden of the Cairn was Lovely Margaret's terrible curse upon her sister brought about.

20. St Columba and the Squirrel

This simple but delightful little wisdom tale was found in Swire's The Inner Hebrides and their Legends. *It is one of very many imaginative stories that tell of St Columba's spiritual journey and is a lesson in forbearance to us all.*

Despite the great powers of faith and miracle-working that Columba, the Abbot of Iona, was so well known for, he was, after all, only a man. Even he was sometimes brought low by feelings of disenchantment and hopelessness. Sometimes he thought all his years of sacrifice and effort had been in vain. He had seen so many converts go back to their pagan ways that the immense task that he had set himself of Christianising all the Scots and the Picts seemed out of reach. In his weakest moments, Columba sometimes thought he should just return to his native home for which he always pined, and there face his own life and struggles.

Suffering such torment as he was, Columba took a boat across to the Isle of Mull and, like Christ, set off into the wilderness to find the solitude he craved, that he might pray and meditate. Eventually his wandering brought him to the shores of Loch Uisg, on the far south-east corner of Mull. The 2-mile-long body of fresh water lying between the pincer-like grip of the two sea lochs Spelvie and Buie blocked his way, or he may have kept on walking a little longer. It was at this remote and beautiful place, surrounded by hills whose slopes were thickly wooded with birch and hazel and oak and rowan trees, that the old monk found what he was looking for.

After many days of prayer and reflection, Columba went down to the water's edge to take a drink. There he came across a squirrel, busily scooping out the water with its little bushy red tail, and he watched intently for a while. When his curiosity got the better of him, he spoke to the squirrel.

'Tell me little one, how is it that you labour so tirelessly?' asked Columba.

'I am trying to empty this loch so I might get to the hazel trees on the far side.'

'But this is an impossible task,' laughed the wise monk. 'You will not live long enough to complete it.'

'True,' said the squirrel, 'but my efforts will make the task a little easier for those who come after me.'

Inspired by his meeting with the little creature of the woods, it was said that Columba returned to Iona. There he renewed his evangelical mission, safe in the knowledge that he was merely laying the foundation stones for those builders of the church who would come long after him.

IONA

21. The Wisdom of St Columba

I have seen whales in the Hebridean Sea, albeit the relatively small and shy minke whale. Their shyness may be due to modern engine noise. In days gone by they may not have been quite so reluctant to approach sail- or oar-powered crafts. In any case, a minke whale surfacing beside a little currach would be a nerve-wracking experience. Of course, there are other whale species to be found here, including the mighty fin and humpback, and probably their numbers were greater centuries ago. The depiction of an encounter between the monks and a whale is perfectly plausible, and maybe St Columba's advice was from his own experience!

The following was compiled from various sources including The Life of St Columba *by Adomnán of Iona (Penguin Classics, 1995). Adomnán was the ninth Abbot of Iona and his account of St Columba's life was written 100 years after the great man's death.*

The old legends say that the little island of Iona was handed over to Colum Cille, the Irish missionary monk who would later become St Columba, by his blood relation, Conall mac Comgaill, then King of Dál Riada.

From Iona, as everyone knows, Columba converted the pagan Gaels and then the Picts to the new religion and became known throughout the Christian world as a holy man and a Christ-like worker of miracles. He was also well known for his ability to forecast everything from the weather to future woes, and his blessing was sought for all undertakings by those who followed him.

At this time the nearby island of Tiree was known as the granary of Iona, for it was as fertile then as it is now, and the monks grew their crops there. Besides this, the monks from Iona had established another monastic settlement on the island.

One day, a monk called Berach came to his Abbot to ask for a blessing to cross the sea to Tiree. Columba answered by telling him to go north-east by Staffa and the north-west coast of Mull, and take the closer crossing to Coll and follow the coast down to Tiree. It was a journey three times as long as a direct passage.

'Why must we take such a long and wearisome voyage, my Reverend Abbot, when to cross the sea as the bird flies would be much the quicker?' queried Berach.

'There is a great sea monster in the channel between here and Tiree, and should your paths cross you will be fortunate to come away with your lives,' replied Columba.

Well, Berach had made the journey many times before and, respectful and obedient as he was, he could not believe that his master could know of such a monster in the vastness of the sea. In quiet defiance of Columba's instructions, Berach lead his men in a currach across the open water to Tiree. Halfway across, a great whale surfaced and its huge back arching through the waves almost overwhelmed their little craft. In great fear of their lives, they watched the beast break the surface of the sea again and again. They prayed fervently and begged God's mercy for their deliverance. At long last the whale sank beneath the waves and eventually they landed safely on Tiree.

The following day another monk called Baithéne, who had accompanied Columba from Ireland and would succeed him as abbot, came to seek his blessing to cross the sea to Tiree. Columba gave him the same warning and instructions.

'Both I and the whale are in God's hands,' replied Baithéne.

'Go in peace then, your faith in Christ will shield you from all danger,' said Columba.

And so, the faithful monk and his companions set out for Tiree in their currach. Again, they met with the whale and again all those aboard were in great fear for their lives. It came so close to their little craft that it threatened to inundate it and send them all to the depths of the ocean. Baithéne alone was undaunted. He stood up in the pitching, rolling currach and, spreading his hands, he called down a blessing over the sea and the whale. With that the giant sea creature disappeared beneath the waves and the surface of the sea was calmed.

Columba's ability, it seemed, to always be right was once again upheld. The many monks and converts who came after him always revered the wisdom of St Columba.

22. The Faerie Mistress of Iona

I found this remarkable story in John Gregorson Campbell's Superstitions of the Highlands and Islands of Scotland. *There are other stories of faerie women who violently abuse their victims, but this is the most interesting and, incidentally, the darkest version I have come across.*

Gregorson Campbell titles this story the 'Iona Bansi'. The role of the banshee (bean sí or bean sidhe) has already been discussed in the introduction to 'The Three Faerie Women'. The faerie woman here appears in a markedly different role, however. She seems to me to be part bean nighe – the washing woman and harbinger of death associated with some very strange folkloric beliefs, and the leannán sídhe *– the faerie lover popularised by the likes of W.B. Yeats in the nineteenth century (see volume cited above for descriptions of both).*

I have taken characteristics from both in an attempt to paint a better description of what Gregorson Campbell refers to at one point as the 'fairy mistress'. For example, the hideousness of the bean nighe *and her wont to answer any question posed to her, contrasted with the irresistible allure of the* leannán sídhe *and her ultimately ruinous effect.*

Iona is best known as the holy island from where St Columba spread Christianity throughout Dál Riada and beyond, but in years gone by unholy things also occurred there.

Once there was an Iona man who was wakened one morning early by the bright light streaming into his little cabin. Thinking dawn was coming, he got up from his bed and went fishing down by the shore. In no time at all he had caught a few fish and decided he would return home. It was only then he realised he had mistaken the bright moonlight for the coming of dawn and, feeling a little tired, he sat down to rest and take a moment under the beautiful moonlit sky.

Very soon he lay back and dozed off to sleep with his hazel fishing rod in one hand and a string of fish in the other. A short time later he was started awake by a tug, tug, tug, on the string of fish and some unseen power trying to wrench the rod from his grasp. The man tightened the grip on his possessions and, a little frightened and bewildered, he rose to his feet to make for home.

As he walked along he became aware of a presence behind him, and then he heard an unearthly weeping and wailing like old keening women at a wake. Petrified now and almost at a run, the man peered over his shoulder. What he saw made his hair stand on end. Coming up behind him was a strange woman not of this world. She was floating, almost, and her long, dark hair flowed out behind her. Her skin was sallow, and her eyes were dark, hollow pools of despair. She appeared as if dressed in a thin, ragged gown through which her sagging breasts were plain to see. In one hand she carried a staff and the other was stretched out toward the man.

'Ask any question and you will be given the answer you want,' she wailed at him.

The man fell to his knees and blessed himself three or more times.

'I put God and Colum Cille between us,' he said with great fervour, but the woman laughed in the face of his piety.

She unleashed an attack on the poor man and beat him mercilessly with her staff until he whimpered like a child. To protect himself, he curled up like an unborn child and prayed for the beating to end. Dawn could not come quickly enough for him, but as soon as the first pink light appeared over the horizon, the otherworldly spirit disappeared and an eerie silence fell.

The man staggered home and barred his door. All day he trembled in his cabin, aching from the beating he had taken.

As night fell, however, he was tempted by some great yearning out into the moonlight again, and again the woman came to him.

'Ask any question and you will be given the answer you want,' she wailed at him and once more he called on the protection of God and Colum Cille, but to no avail. If he had been beaten sorely the night before, this time the faerie woman flailed him until he was black and blue all over. Night after night it was the same, until the man had no choice but flee the island of Iona and seek sanctuary on the mainland. To his blessed relief, the night visitations ceased – for a while.

One day he was working for a farmer cutting turf in a bog. Taking a spell of rest, he looked up and there on the bank he saw a raven watching him. He tried to scare it away, but the bird was fearless. Then the man knew this was his tormentor. That night he was drawn like the tide by the full moon to meet with her again, and with her staff she beat him once more.

In desperation the man made up his mind that he would make his escape to Ireland. Surely, he thought, she would not follow him across the sea. On the night before his departure, he was powerless to resist the lure of the faerie woman, and he went out to meet her once more by the light of the full moon.

'You think to run away from me, but when you reach Erin's shore the first creature to greet you will be a hoodie crow. That crow will be me.'

She cackled and laughed at the poor man's misery. Nowhere on Earth could he find peace or refuge from his faerie mistress, for always he was drawn to her. In the end, one night under the full moon, she killed him.

TIREE

23. The Brownie of Baugh

The brownies or broonies of Scottish folklore are closely related to the grugagh (the latter being found in Irish folklore also) and, to a lesser extent, the glastaig. Variously these otherworldly or faerie creatures are a help to humans and take on a servant's role — brownies and grugaghs most commonly identifying as male and glastaigs as female. They can all be mischievous when it comes to playing tricks on, for example, lackadaisical human servants. They require recompense for their efforts in the form of milk or cream left out by the household, and are notoriously very easily offended.

On the very rare occasions when brownies and grugaghs are seen by humans, they often appear as little hairy folk, half dressed in rags or completely naked. In the case of glastaigs, which are more often seen, they appear as small, unattractive women with very long hair, but can sometimes take other forms. If the human beholder is, for instance, prompted by pity to offer new clothes or footwear, then the faerie in question will refuse and promptly withdraw their succour never to be seen or heard tell of again. Glastaigs can become more of a spiteful nuisance in these circumstances.

Similar otherworldly creatures are found all over Europe and frequently appear in folk tales. 'The Elves and the Shoemaker' of Grimms Fairy Tales *comes most readily to mind.*

The makings of this tale came from McGregor's The Peat Fire Flame.

For long many a day the folk of Tiree have tilled the fertile soils and reaped bountiful crops on that jewel of an island. The ploughing and the sowing and harrowing was all hard work, of course, but the most wearisome task of all was to keep livestock away from the land cultivated by the islanders. During the day it was not so difficult for a young lad or lassie to keep an eye on the sheep or cattle. At night, however, when the moon waned, the job demanded constant vigilance. A cowherd's inattention could end up in a whole season's labour being undone.

Years ago, in the townland of Baugh near the south shore of Tiree, the folk round about had no such worry, for in that vicinity there lived a brownie. As long as anyone could remember, this little creature had taken upon itself the duties of the herdsman. From sunset to sunrise the Brownie of Baugh watched over the animals and never an ear of wheat nor leaf of green kale was so much as nibbled. All the folk ever did to maintain the understanding was to leave the brownie a wee sup of fresh milk every evening in a bowl-shaped stone set out for the job.

Doubtless an odd gull had kept a watch to try and see the brownie for himself. But all down the years not a single mortal soul had ever caught a glimpse, for it was as invisible as it was constant. Mostly the folk were content to leave well enough alone for every poor farmer knows never to look a gift horse in the mouth.

But then one time a man who was said to be blessed with the gift of second sight stayed out all night, and in the morning he told all and sundry that he had laid eyes on the brownie.

'He was a little fella about the size of a hare,' he said, 'and damn near as hairy. He wore barely a stitch of clothing on his back and not a shoe to his foot. When the cattle went too near the crops he called softly and, with a sally rod for a switch, he herded them away down to the machair to graze on the wildflowers and grasses by the shore.'

The people were in awe of what the man had seen, though some were disbelieving.

'Did he see you?' asked one sharply.

'He did,' stammered the man blessed with the second sight. 'And– and I spoke to him, for I felt a pity on the wee fella, the night was that cold. I offered to get him brogues for his feet and a pair of new britches.'

'And did he answer ye?' asked another of the farmers with his eyes out on stalks now.

'He did,' said the man. 'He told me his name and voiced his displeasure in a rhyme.'

'Not for Gunna shoes or breeks
'And Gunna at the farmer's chore
'The man with second sight misspeaks,
'I'll ne'er herd the cattle more.'
]

With these lines of verse, Gunna, the Brownie of Baugh, took his leave, and the man who saw him was left to ponder the offence he had caused. Ever since the people of that townland were obliged to do their own cattle herding at night and curse the man blessed with second sight.

COLONSAY

24. McPhee and the Seal

Found in Swire's The Inner Hebrides and their Legends, *this is an extraordinary tale from the island of Colonsay with a dramatic twist on the traditional 'selkie story'. It is quite well known and appears in various collections of folk tales, including an interesting adaptation in* Strange Tales of the Western Isles *by Halbert J. Boyd (Eanas McKay, Stirling, 1930).*

The central character bears the family name McPhee, whose members are traditionally said to be the descendants of seal-folk: the so-called selkies. It is said that McPhees are often born with syndactyly – tissue connecting two or more fingers or toes; that is to say, webbing.

McPhee's hound is an interesting motif in the story – is it just a fearsome but otherwise ordinary canine, or some class of faerie dog similar, for example, to that found in the story 'Kaelin the Wanderer'?

There was once many years ago a fisherman by the name of McPhee who lived on the island of Colonsay. It was long known that folk bearing that name were descendants of a seal-woman who had been held against her will, or at least her nature, until she somehow recovered her own seal skin and returned to the sea. But that was many years before.

One fine day McPhee went fishing around the island in his currach. Suddenly he was struck by an angry squall, and a rogue wave capsized the small vessel. Unusually for an islander, McPhee was a strong swimmer but, weighed down by his heavy woollen garb, he floundered in the cold water. His life flashed before his eyes as he sunk down into the depths and a great feeling of warmth and peace came over him.

He was rudely shaken from his reverie, however, when a seal suddenly took hold of him and hauled him through the water and into a cave further along the shore. With the seal's help, McPhee dragged himself up onto a small sandy beach at the back of the cave.

By now he was feeling the effects of his ordeal, and he shivered with the cold and shock, and all the while the seal watched him from the water. Suddenly it disappeared, but returned a short time later with a fish and, much to McPhee's amazement, it showed no fear but came up onto the beach beside him. McPhee was grateful to the seal, for it had saved his life. He began to speak to the animal as if it understood his every word and might answer but, as intelligent and knowing as its big eyes seemed to be, it made no reply.

As the tide rose, McPhee moved further up into the cave and the seal followed. That night it lay beside McPhee and kept him warm. It sang its eerie seal songs in that rocky chamber and at first McPhee's hair stood on end. After a while he grew to find them very beautiful and comforting.

The next day passed in much the same way and the seal attended to McPhee's needs, but he had recovered his strength and wished to return to his wife and young family. When he told the seal this, hoping she might somehow understand and perhaps assist him again, she thrashed the water with her fins and bared her fierce teeth. It was the same every time McPhee moved towards the entrance of the cave. He soon realised the seal meant to keep him as some sort of prisoner.

I do not know how long McPhee was held captive like this, but one day when the seal was away for food, he stripped off his clothes and slipped into the water. When he got outside the cave, he began to swim for his life. Just as he neared the shore, he heard the seal dashing through the waves behind him. He made the beach just before she caught up with him, but as he found his shaking legs on the land and began to run, tripping and falling all the way, she came after him with surprising speed, snarling and baring her ferocious fangs.

Well, he didn't have to run far before his home came into view. McPhee began to call for his faithful dog. It was a vicious black brute of a hound and in truth everyone on the island was petrified of it. McPhee's wife had often begged him to destroy the thing before it attacked a child, or some other tragedy occurred, but McPhee loved the animal.

'Every dog has its day, and that black dog will have his,' he always said.

When the dog heard its master's cries for help, it broke free from its chain and ran towards the sound. It reached McPhee at the same instant as the seal and the two animals joined in mortal combat. Hair and skin and blood flew as they tore great lumps of flesh from one another's throats. They snarled and yelped and cried, but they were a match for each other – one driven by loyalty and love, the other by fury and jealousy. McPhee could only look on helplessly and in horror as his beloved dog was viciously wounded, while in turn it worried the seal savagely.

In the end, both animals lay dead in a great pool of blood and gore. Heartbroken and shaken, but grateful for his life, McPhee returned to his family. For the rest of his long life, he always shuddered to imagine what might have happened that day if it hadn't been for the strength and courage of his beloved big black dog.

25. The Faithful Runt

This is just one of several stories I have found about the Colonsay McPhees and their hounds. This may be my favourite. It is eerie, poignant and heartwarming all at the same time. It is also to be found in Swire's The Inner Hebrides and their Legends *under the title 'The Spectre of Colonsay'. The title was changed as I thought the story to be more about the character of the hound than the ghost.*

In this story I think the hound is less of a faerie dog and more of this world, with ordinary dog-like senses and old-fashioned loyalty. The trajectory of its journey from being perceived as a useless runt to the dog who saves the day is reminiscent of that followed by many reluctant hero-type characters.

As well as their close and well-known ties to the seal-folk, the McPhees of Colonsay always had a great interest in dogs and dog breeding. This was certainly true of one McPhee in particular, who was very proud of his own strain of hound. Of course, there were always runts in every litter that had to be done away with. The McPhees, however, always preferred to give every dog the chance to have its day.

This one time McPhee had a litter, and he reared them all up to be big young dogs. Some were better than others, but one bitch in particular was of no use at all. It never took to hunting or guarding the beasts and neither would it bark as a good watchdog should. It was gentle and went about with a hump on its back licking stranger's hands.

'That dog has eaten enough meat,' McPhee said one day.

'Let me keep her,' said his cook. 'She's more clever than you think.'

'Very well,' said McPhee. 'Let her lie by the fire and eat scraps. That's all she's fit for.'

The cook had grown very fond of the dog and was happy when his master relented, though in truth McPhee was glad of the excuse, for he disliked having to do away with any of his dogs.

One night McPhee had strayed longer than intended and was coming back from the hill late in the evening. Clouds drifted across the moon, and it grew so dark that he became unsure of the way and regretted not coming home earlier. As he stumbled about trying to find the track, he suddenly felt a cold breeze on his cheeks, which was odd, for there was not a breath of wind and the evening was fine.

Suddenly he saw a strange shimmering light coming towards him, and in an instant he knew that he was facing the Ghost of Colonsay – a shapeless otherworldly being who appeared to unwary travellers at night. Who or what this spirit was no one knew, but to all it appeared death followed soon after. Mercifully, it was a rare visitor, but on every occasion a single life and no more was taken.

McPhee thought of fleeing, but in his heart of hearts he knew he could not outrun his fate. In any case, his legs were weak, and it was too dark to find his way. Closer and closer the light came, and McPhee tried to be brave, but cold fear was coursing through his body and he trembled uncontrollably. Just then he felt the brush of soft fur on the back of his hand as something passed by him at great speed. The clouds parted just then and by the faint light of the moon McPhee saw that it was the cook's pet – the bitch whose life he had spared only to lie by the fire.

Now it leapt at the shimmering light, putting itself between the spirit and McPhee. Alas, it fell down stone dead in mid-air without so much as a whimper. In that instant the strange light faded and the night air became warm and pleasant once more. McPhee could only imagine that the spirit, content with the one stolen life of a dog, had returned to the dark place from which it came.

McPhee eventually got home, carrying the body of the faithful dog in his arms. Never again did he give the slightest thought to doing away with any runt, no matter how much of a weakling it seemed to be.

26. McPhee and Dounhulia

This story appears in a lengthy dissertation by K. MacLeay entitled, Description of Spar Cave, *published in 1811 and subsequently in* Swire's Skye, The Island and its Legends. *The former contains a more comprehensive version of the story.*

Despite the fact that the heroine comes from Skye and a lot of the action takes place there, I have reframed it as a Colonsay story on the grounds that it features a McPhee and his dog, who are synonymous with that island, and also because it starts and finishes there.

The Spar Cave refers to an actual place, largely despoiled now, its stalactites and stalagmites having been taken as souvenirs or ground down to make lime for the land. It remains a tourist attraction for other geological features that survive.

There was once a son of the McPhee of Colonsay who, like all his kin, never strayed far without his beloved hound. The animal was his most faithful friend and guardian. Good a dog as it was, it could not save his master when an Ulster chieftain called MacCairbre came to Colonsay, intent on demanding fealty from his father. To show good faith, McPhee gave the Ulsterman his son to take away and teach the arts of war.

The Ulsterman and his warriors were on their way home after plundering all they could find further north as far as the Isle of Skye. While the lords and protectors of Skye were away fighting against the Picts under a Viking chief, MacCairbre had cut down all who stood in his path. When the Skye men returned to news that MacCairbre had been pillaging unopposed up and down the coast, they determined to sail for Erin and take their revenge. This they duly did with a hundred-strong fleet of birlinns. Upon reaching Ulster, a fierce battle ensued, and much blood was spilled. In the end, MacCairbre was slain, and the Skye men triumphed, but it was at a high price to both sides.

Young Colonsay and his hound were taken prisoner and carried off to Skye as the spoils of war. On their journey home, the Skye men were beset by a terrible storm and all their ships were lost. One birlinn managed to get into the calmer waters of Loch Slapin on the south coast of Skye, but was wrecked there. From the shore a young woman called Dounhulia, the daughter of the local Dunglas chieftain, saw the ship coming to grief and sent men to rescue whomever they could. When so many had drowned it was nothing but a wonder that young McPhee of Colonsay and his faithful hound survived.

When the local chieftain discovered a McPhee among the survivors, he swallowed a bitter taste in his mouth, for he and the young man's father had crossed swords in the past and no love was lost between them. 'Perhaps a ransom would be paid by this scrawny brat's kin,' thought the old man to himself. Knowing the McPhee's regard for their dogs, he bid to throw the hound into the bargain. In the meantime, while word was sent and a reply awaited, both were held as prisoners.

Despite her father's misgivings, the chieftain's daughter began to pay visits to the young McPhee and his hound in their dreary chamber. With little else to occupy or excite them, the young couple became very close. Days became weeks and the weeks became months and in time a baby son was born to the lovely Dounhulia. Fearing her father's wrath should he discover that a McPhee had fathered his bastard grandchild, Dounhulia and her child fled, taking her maid, McPhee, and his hound to a place called the Spar Cave.

The cavern was famous for the strange shapes that hung down like giant stone icicles and the great spikes that pointed contrarywise up towards the vaulted ceiling. The walls glistened and sparkled like snow and ice on a winter's night and the place was said to be haunted by merfolk whose echoing songs could drive men to madness. Deep in this otherworldly dwelling, the little family took refuge and McPhee's hound lay siege to the entrance so that no man or wild beast would dare to enter.

With Dounhulia's help, McPhee soon escaped and returned to Colonsay, though he left his faithful hound to guard his lover and their child. There he set about convincing his father that a marriage between him and Dounhulia would mend the old bad blood dividing their two clans. For her part, Dounhulia did likewise and swayed her father's mind. To cut a long story short, both their fathers eventually saw the futility of opposing such a match and the couple were not long to be wed.

Dounhulia, her husband and child and the maid all went to Colonsay where, by all accounts, they lived quite happily guarded, as always, by McPhee's faithful hound.

THE CORRYVRECKAN

27. The Whirlpool of Breacan

Positioned at the centre of Dál Riada, it seems fitting that a story about the mighty Corryvrecken should be put right in the middle of this book. There are several folk tales surrounding the formation and/or naming of this amazing tidal phenomenon. In the body of this rendering, it is referred to as the Churn of the Old Hag – Old Hag being an Cailleach, but that's another story.

The Corryvrecken is the third most powerful whirlpool in the world. The Saltstraumen Maelstrom in Nordland, Norway, and the Old Sow in the bay of Fundy, Canada, come in at number one and two respectively. Twice I have been scheduled to go and visit the Corryvrecken and twice the weather has had other ideas.

This is my favourite Corryvrecken tale, for it has everything – a love tryst, a brave hero, a quest, deceit and disaster! The following has been compiled from various sources, most notably Swire's The Inner Hebrides and their Legends.

Brecan was a Lochlann prince from a time now long passed. A beautiful daughter of the Lord of the Isles had caught his eye and for her his heart yearned and his body ached. The Lord of the Isles, however, had other plans for his daughter's future. Nevertheless, the great chieftain did not wish to incur the wrath of the King of Lochlann by refusing to allow the marriage between his daughter and the Norseman's son. In the hope that it would avoid offence, he devised a plan to thwart Brecan's ambitions.

'Nothing would please me more than a union between the royal house of Lochlann and my own clan, but before any marriage can take place you must prove yourself,' said the wily old chieftain.

'I will do anything,' replied Brecan from the bottom of his heart.

'To marry my daughter and one day become Lord of the Isles, you must first show that you have mastery over all the seas. To do this, you will anchor yourself in the great Churn of the Old Hag and there remain for three days and three nights.'

Knowing no fear, Brecan sailed straight away for his homeland. There he begged his father's best longship and finest crew. Before he left to face the Churn of the Old Hag, he consulted his father's wisemen. They were dismayed that the prince should undertake such a perilous venture, but they could not counsel against him.

'You must make three cables,' their eldest advised. 'The first must be of wool shorn from first-year lambs. The second from the fibres of nettles grown in a graveyard. The third must be woven from the hair of thousand virgins – beware Brecan, every hair of it must be from the head of a fair and true maiden, or ruin will follow.'

Hoping the last cable would be impossible to make, the wise men sent Brecan away on his quest. The first two cables were easily enough made. The last proved more difficult, but not impossible, for the prince was handsome and beloved by every maid in the land. Knowing the endeavour was to win the prince a wife, and in hopes of gaining his favour, maidens from every corner of Lochlann clamoured to bequeath their hair. Soon the third cable was finished, and with his father's blessing and a fine ship under him, Brecan set sail for the Churn of the Old Hag.

Not long after, his ship came within sight of the surging, raging waters. While the tide was slack, and with great skill, the ship was positioned at the heart of the eerily peaceful current. Only then was she secured by the three cables. The Norsemen braced themselves for the churning and swirling tempest that would surely come. For a day and a night the longship was tossed about like a leaf in a billowing torrent. Suddenly the woollen cable snapped. The ship lurched around violently and all aboard thought she was lost, but the last two cables held fast.

Another day and a night passed and not a single man could keep the contents of his stomach down, though they were hardened seamen that had seen many a tempest. Suddenly the cable made from nettle fibres snapped, the ship pitched up on her bow and the crew had to cling on for fear they would be thrown into the raging swirling waters.

On the third day Brecan felt that, although the waters still raged about them and their ship was yet in peril, the Churn of the Old Hag was a little less angry. But then one of the hairs on the third cable broke. With all the strain on that one cable, it soon came undone. In a few moments it unravelled and Brecan's ship was sucked down into the cruel swirling depths of that maelstrom. But for that one maiden who had played Brecan false the cable would have held, and the Lochlann prince would have gained the Lord of the Isles' daughter for his wife.

From that day onwards people called that treacherous seaway between Jura and the island of Scarba the Whirlpool of Breacan – the Corryvrecken. The only living thing to come out of the sea that day was Brecan's faithful hound. By some means it had been thrown clear and made it to shore. Devoted dog that it was, it sniffed the air and plunged straight back in. It somehow managed to find its master and dragged his body to shore.

With a shake of its coat, it again dashed into the freezing water to, it is thought, bring more of Brecan's men to shore. Alas, the currents proved too strong even for such a heartsome hound and it was never seen more. They say it was washed out to sea and in its efforts to swim back it stirred up the little Corryvrecken or the Grey Dog's whirlpool, a lesser known but unnavigable current between Scarba and the beautiful island of Lunga where the seabirds come to breed in summer.

Brecan was buried on the north shore of Jura, for they say those taken by the sea should be buried within her reach. Near a cave that still bears his name, a cairn was raised over his grave and there it stood for many years. Wind and wave have long since torn it asunder and now the exact site is lost to memory. Brecan's name, however, will always be remembered through the story of the Corryvrecken.

JURA

28. Kaelin the Wanderer

Folk tales from Jura seem to be a little thin on the ground and there were not many to choose from. Perhaps this is because Jura was never so well populated as its close neighbour, Islay. Had there been hundreds of Jura folk tales, though, I would still have chosen this one. It has mystery, murder and mayhem in abundance. The villains get their comeuppance and the hero, and his dog, live to fight another day – all very satisfying for the listener or reader.

Jura is a truly beautiful island, perhaps best known and loved for her mountains or Paps – breasts in Gaelic. These are especially pretty when clad with snow and visible for many miles across the sea and from every part of Dál Riada.

I have developed this story from a sketch found in Swire's The Inner Hebrides and their Legends.

On the Island of Jura many years ago there lived a young man called Kaelin. His mother died when he was but a child, and his chieftain father remarried and had another family of twelve sons. Even so, Kaelin was always his favourite and was to be his heir.

Having twelve stepbrothers and a stepmother who cared much less for him, Kaelin never felt part of his father's second family. He was always a loner with the heart of a wanderer. Often he climbed Beinn an Òir – Mountain of Gold – the highest of the Paps of Jura, and from there surveyed the surrounding seas and islands. It was from here that he vowed to himself that one day he would sail the swirling seas and set foot on those seemingly distant lands.

When Kaelin came of age he did as he had always dreamed, setting out from Jura to find his way in the world, and many were the adventures he had. During one voyage his ship was wrecked in a storm and Kaelin was fortunate to come ashore on an unknown island. He was more dead than alive, but he was found washed up on the white beach by an old woman. She took him home and cared for him until he slowly regained his strength and wits.

Eventually Kaelin became well and fit enough to leave. After many years of travelling, a great urge to return to Jura came upon him. Not knowing how he might get home, and with few possessions other than the clothes on his back, he bid his farewell to the woman who had saved his life.

'Will you accept one last gift from me Kaelin?' she said.

'You have done so much for me already,' he said. 'I am by now deep in your debt.'

'Take this and your debts will be repaid,' she said, and she gave Kaelin a black whelp.

Wondering to himself how he would ever keep the young dog alive, but not wishing to offend the woman, he took it under his care without question or query and gave thanks.

'He will be more faithful than any ordinary hound if you are faithful to him,' said the old woman. With that she bid Kaelin good fortune and let him leave.

To cut a long story short, Kaelin eventually made his way back to the island of his birth and ancestors. He was saddened to hear news of his father's death and, moreover, wounded by the cold welcome he received from his stepmother and twelve stepbrothers. The lands his father left were rightfully his, but Kaelin has been thought dead and gone, never to set foot on Jura again. His unexpected return had set a fox among the fowl.

While Kaelin trustingly prepared to receive his birthright and settle back down to life on Jura, his stepbrothers plotted murder against him. They could not agree which of them should carry out the dreadful deed. So, one night all twelve came together, each intent on bloodying their hands and their blades that all might bear the guilt equally. Kaelin was unsuspecting, but not so his faithful black dog, who by now was a great fearsome beast that never left his master's side. As the assassins approached under cover of darkness, the dog attacked. By the time Kaelin had roused himself and realised what was happening all twelve of his stepbrothers lay dead – their throats torn out.

Just as the woman had foretold, Kaelin's dog was more faithful than any ordinary hound for, of course, it was a faerie dog. Then again, like all gifts from the faerie folk, the dog was attended by a curse – Kaelin himself was accused of murdering his own kinsfolk. Other clansmen hungry for his land saw the opportunity and came, supposedly, to avenge their deaths.

Kaelin fled his island home to become a wanderer once more. Many years he searched for the unknown island on which he had been rescued by the woman, but he never found it or her again. And though Kaelin often travelled without man or woman for company, he was never alone in this world, for always he had his companion by his side – the faithful faerie hound.

ISLAY

29. The Swan of Good Fortune

Among the many legends and folkloric beliefs surrounding these birds was one holding that swans were virtuous women under evil enchantment. Another said that to see seven swans flying together was a sure sign of seven years of plenty to come. Since ancient times it has been believed that to do a swan any harm would bring misfortune.

This narrative bears a striking similarity to a traditional Cree story found in Hugh Lupton's beautiful book, Tales of Wisdom and Wonder *(Barefoot Books Ltd, 2000) under the title 'The Curing Fox'. Did the story travel or did it emerge simultaneously in two entirely different cultures? I do not have the answer to this intriguing question. I discovered this story in McGregor's* The Peat Fire Flame, *but – unusually – he does not indicate where he found it. Rightly or wrongly, I have attributed it to the island of Islay.*

Here I have taken the liberty of incorporating a similar question to that posed by Lupton at the conclusion of his rendering of 'The Curing Fox'.

A long time ago, in a small cabin built of mud and thatched with marram grass, a woman nursed her sickly young daughter. For weeks the little girl had been ill while her fever raged like a fire. Her skin burned red hot, kept cool only by the constant laying on of cloths moistened by cold spring water, and her wee lips were parched and cracked. All brews and remedies had failed, and as her young life ebbed away her broken hearted mother prepared to mourn another one of her children.

Early one morning in April, the woman was down gathering shellfish along the shore at low tide, for she still had other children to feed. As she worked her way along the water's edge, she came across a swan, weakened in some way and unable to fly. The poor creature lay helpless on the beach with its neck stretched out and its eyes closed.

The woman had heard the old stories about swans and that some were maidens under evil enchantments, but she had also heard that a swan had strength enough to break a man's arm with one sweep of its wing. Even so, she knelt beside the great bird and laid her hands on its white feathers. The swan barely stirred. Then the woman bravely put her thin arms around its body and with all her strength raised it from the stony beach. The swan made no effort to resist, but it was heavy and the woman laboured under its weight. She stopped many times to lay down her load that she might catch her breath and ease the aching in her arms.

When she got back to her cabin, the woman made the swan a bed of straw and bound up its wings, for one hung down limply and was plainly wounded. With great patience, she fed the bird flakes of barley and offered it drops of fresh spring water. For days it barely moved, but then one morning when the woman awoke she saw that the swan had found its big black leathery feet again and was standing strong. Its long neck stretched upwards, and it was lively and watchful.

That morning the little girl's fever broke. The moment her eyes opened she turned her head and, not showing the slightest surprise, beheld the swan with great interest. From then on she barely took her gaze away from the huge white bird.

The swan began eating and drinking of its own accord. As it did, the woman noticed something that lifted the cold weight of dread from her heart. Her sickly daughter began to take her first sips of milk and little mouthfuls of porridge. As the swan mended, so too did the child. Before long she was sitting up in bed, always watching the swan with great fascination as the bird stared back.

Eventually, the woman unbound the swan's wing. To the child's sheer delight, it stretched its great white cloak once again, filling the cabin with a cool breeze and stirring the peats glowing on the hearth. One morning the mother found her daughter curled up and asleep under the swan's wing, the bird's long neck around hers like a fine white feather scarf. It was the same every morning after that.

The woman began to let the swan out to graze on the fresh green shoots of grass beginning to show round about, and from the doorway of the cabin the little girl watched intently. By the end of May she was well enough to go outside herself and follow the swan here and there. One morning, hand in hand with her mother, she skipped along as the swan paddled its way down the rushing brown burn to the sea. There it opened it wings and gracefully took off into the wind. To the delight of the woman and the little girl, screeching with excitement, it scribed one great low arc in the sky and swept noisily over their heads before it flew off into the far blue distance.

To her dying day the woman firmly believed that the swan to which she had devoted so much time and care had been endowed with magical powers or was otherwise enchanted. In return, the bird had bestowed good fortune on her and her children. It was true that never again did ill health or untimely death darken that family's door, but the question always haunted the woman – did the swan really cure the child, or was it the child that cured the swan?

30. The Swan Maiden of Islay

Swans have been a common sight around our coastlines for as long as anyone can remember. They appear in river mouths, sheltered bays and sea loughs all along the coast. They are often to be seen flying wing tip to wing tip in formations across the sky. Where they gather in great numbers, they always grant us one of the most beautiful spectacles in nature.

Just as in the previous story, some of these birds were, of course, not swans at all. In the folklore, a very special few were said to be swan maidens who, on occasion, took the shape of a young woman. In this human form they were just as beautiful and pure in appearance as when dressed in their garb of white plumage. It's a very similar premise of the classic selkie folk tale with a just hint of 'The Children of Lir'.

I developed this story from the version found in Swire's The Inner Hebrides and their Legends. *An adaptation also appears in Tom Muir's* Tales of Viking Lands *(Orcadian Ltd, 2014) and is said to be a tale of Swedish origin.*

One fine evening in May on the island of Islay, a young man was walking along the banks of the Laggan River hoping to spy an early-run salmon. As he made his way, he kept to the shadows as much as possible. In the undergrowth he came across a great cape of white feathers with the wings and all attached. Not really knowing what it was, but being intrigued all the more for that, he gathered it up neatly and stowed it in a sack he had brought with him to hold any fish he might have hooked with his gaff.

A little further on he saw what he thought was a wraith or a faerie woman. He froze to the spot in terror. What his eyes beheld in the half-light was not a spirit, but a maiden wandering along the bank, trailing her hands behind her through the ferns and grasses. Her eyes were closed in careless rapture and her head was thrown back in abandon as she breathed in the evening air. She was, from top to toe, stark naked. Her long, flaxen hair seemed to float on the gentle breeze. Her skin was as white as snow and her lips the colour of a rowan berry. In that instant the young man became completely besotted by her, for he had never seen the likes before.

As you might imagine, he took a quare eyeful before he accidentally betrayed his presence by breaking a twig under his tread. The maiden came instantly to the alert. Like a startled animal, she darted one way and then the other. She was trying to get back to where she had left her mantle of feathers. Without it she could not transform herself back into a swan.

Eventually, the young man got close enough to offer the maiden his coat and reassure her that he meant her no harm. He spoke softly to her and gently took her hand. In the gathering dusk he walked her to his home overlooking the sea. To cut a long story short, he fell passionately in love with her, and they set up home together as man and wife. Eventually, they had three beautiful children and by all accounts and outward appearances the family were as happy as could be.

Time passed and the children grew stronger and more bold. One day they were playing further along the shore than they ever had before, when they came across a small cave. Egged on by her older siblings, the youngest girl crept into it and there she found a sack. She called to the rest, thinking she had found some treasure stashed by a fearful islander fleeing a Viking raid. The children were wild with excitement and ran home to show their mother.

When the sack was opened, the woman let out a cry of anguish that would have wakened the dead. She buried her face in her hands and wept bitterly at the sight of the strange cape of beautiful white feathers. The children were completely distraught. The loudest noise they had ever heard was their own laughter. They had rarely heard their mother upset about anything and never had they seen her weep.

When their father came home he found the fire dead and the cabin in darkness. There was no fresh baked bread or evening meal prepared. Nor was there the sound of happy children around the table. He found them cowering in a corner of the wee one-roomed cabin, whimpering and sobbing.

'What the Devil's wrong?' he asked them. 'Where's your mother?'

They could hardly tell him for the tears that streamed down their cheeks, but eventually, word by painful word, they explained how their mother had bid them farewell. How she had taken off her clothes and donned the strange cloak of white feathers. How she had spread her wings just like a wild swan and then flew off into the wind. They had watched her for a long time until she was completely out of sight.

The young man instantly fell into a melancholy state of mind. Not even his children had the power over their father to bring him around. Eventually his sister and her husband took the children and reared them, for their father was barely fit to look after himself, never mind them. Somehow or other

he survived, scraping a living along the shore. Always on his mind was the swan maiden who had long ago appeared to him as if in a dream.

Many years passed like this, but one autumn a very strange thing happened. Among the formations of swans returning from the north was a small flock, more tightly packed than the rest. Between them they carried something. When they landed near the lonely cabin where the man and his happy family had once lived, one of them shrugged off its feathers and transformed into a beautiful woman. She walked up the beach while her companions waited. Carrying a mantle of pure white feathers draped over her arm, she approached the cabin and there she found her husband – much older now and sitting by the cold hearth with his head in his hands. She helped him to take off his clothes and dress in the mantle of feathers. He was transformed into a magnificent cob swan and together they went down to the water and flew away into the evening sky.

And that would have been the end of the story, except that years later – some say a hundred, some say two hundred – one Sunday morning as the people went to church, a lone swan returned to that place where the cabin once stood. Now it was in ruins, the chimney gone and the rafters long since rotted away. The swan landed and shrugged off its mantle of white feathers to reveal a man with pale skin and dark hair.

He closed his eyes and scented the air, and a faint smile played about his lips. Suddenly the church bell rang. The moment that sound reached his ears, the man's skin began to shrivel, and his hair turned white as snow. His back bowed into a stoop and from that he fell to a skeleton that turned to fine dust and blew away on the wind.

31. The Faerie's Wisdom

I also found this delightful little story in Swire's The Inner Hebrides *and their Legends and have had much fun retelling it to various audiences. At the end of the tale is an old saying, a version of which I recalled hearing when I was growing up.*

Swire framed the story with a heavy emphasis on the female cast. I have taken the liberty of reimagining both sexes as equally lacking and therefore in need of wisdom. Otherwise, I stayed quite close to Swire's version.

A thousand or maybe two thousand years ago people were no different than today. They were oftentimes very foolish. In the old Kingdom of Dál Riada, clan fought against clan and brother against brother. The queen of the faerie folk, who lived on Islay at the heart of the kingdom, was worried that the people might destroy themselves entirely. So, she decided to do something about it.

She gave orders to let it be known that she was going to bestow a special gift upon her human neighbours. Word was carried across the sea by the wind and the waves. Fish brought news up the rivers and the birds and beasts fetched it through the woods. Even the leaves on the trees and the grasses whispered of the great event.

Throughout the entire Kingdom of Dál Riada, people went to a certain faerie hill on a certain day at a certain time. The hill was opened and the people streamed in. They were dumbfounded by the splendour of the faerie residence. The walls were covered with shimmering, brightly coloured butterfly wings. Candles of beeswax filled the cavernous halls with light and the smell of summer. No one had ever come across the likes of it before – at least no one who had returned to tell the tale.

When everyone was assembled, the faeries closed the doors and the festivities began. There were pipers and harpists and fiddlers. The faerie folk went round every one of their guests with tiny goblets no bigger than a thimble, and from little flagons they dispensed a fiery liquid. To each man and woman they gave just a dram and no more.

'Drink up, drink up,' the faerie queen called.

The people knew fine well that they were not supposed to take anything from the faeries lest they be unable to return to their own world. On this one occasion they had been assured that there would be no trickery.

'What drink is this?' the people asked, for they had never tasted the likes before.

'It is distilled wisdom held in oak casks for a thousand years. It will fortify ye against pride and prejudice and all kinds of foolishness,' cried the wee folk.

Well, as you can imagine, some people didn't trust the faeries and were nervous about drinking this potent otherworldly brew. But some drank their own and half of their neighbour's share as well.

While the last few drops were being poured out, a great disturbance could be heard outside. It was like a continuous rumbling roar of thunder. Inside the faerie hill the people cowered in dread, but the wee folk bid them to have no fear. Only when the doors were reopened to let the people go home did the source of the commotion become plain. It was all the other people who had come too late and couldn't get in. They had been left outside behind the closed doors and were running around trying to find the entrance. Alas, there was no wisdom left, and the latecomers were turned away.

It was this event that gave rise to a common saying. This was rendered into English from the Gaelic and has come down to us from that ancient time. It is used to refer to someone who is a bit foolish or otherwise lacking in wit. When I was young I often heard the old folk say about such a poor person, 'God love him, he must have been behind the door when the faeries were handing out the wisdom.'

32. The Lady of the Emerald Isle

Well known in Irish and Scottish folklore (and virtually every island has account of one) faerie winds and, perhaps, just as commonly, faerie waves, are similarly counteracted by throwing iron blades – knives, axes and or reaping hooks – into them. This action usually also requires the quoting of some words along the lines of, 'This is for you, give me what is mine.'

In essence, this is a changeling story with the added dramatic imagery of the faerie wind. I developed the story from a much-condensed sketch in McGregor's The Peat Fire Flame, *fleshing out the narrative to make it more complete and flow better with, hopefully, a more satisfying conclusion. Although I introduced the Rathlin Island connection, it remains an Islay story.*

The month of May is always a beautiful time of year. But in the North Channel that separates Rathlin Island from the Mull of Kintyre and Islay, there can also be sudden bouts of stormy weather with swirling winds as dreaded as any winter gale.

A long time ago on the island of Islay, a young girl by the name of Morag was betrothed to an island farmer. All summer long, however, she was secretly courted by a handsome lad from Rathlin called Ruairi.

Only half a day's sailing separated their island homes. When Ruairi came over, which was as often as he could, he would pull his currach up on to the sand and the pair would go walking together along the southern shore of the Oa of Islay.

'Where will we live when we're married my love?' she would ask Ruiari.

'On Rachery,' he always replied as he pointed across the sea to his native island on the southern horizon.

A year and a day passed, and their love took its course. In the month of May, Morag's waist began to swell. When her mother broke the news to her father, he wanted to have Ruiari's life.

'Ah, give over,' Morag's mother scolded. 'It's a very short memory you have. Morag's not the first and she won't be the last.'

Nothing could be done except hastily arrange a wedding. Ruairi's people came over from Rathlin to join in the festivities. And for all the bad temper and bluster of Morag's father, a grand time was had by all.

The following day, the newly-weds went for one last walk along the southern shore of the Oa. The weather was warm and fine and there was a gentle breeze coming off the sea.

'Tell me again my love,' said Morag. 'Where will we live now that we're married?'

As Ruairi pointed across the sea, the two young lovers noticed an eddy of wind coming over the water. It twisted and swirled around and whipped the surface of the sea into white horses. The nearer it came, the bigger and more violent it seemed to become. When it made land they could feel the swirl of cold air and taste the salt sea spray. Pieces of driftwood and rocks were lifted by it and flung up into the air. As it bore down on the young couple, Morag was struck on the head by something and fell to the ground. Ruairi was swept up into that swirling mass of air and thrown about like a rag.

When Morag regained her senses she looked about, but Ruairi was nowhere to be seen. Then she found him lying in the grass a hundred yards away. His clothes were tattered and torn, and he was greatly changed. The colour had drained from his cheeks. The spark had gone out of his eyes. He was a shadow of the lively young man he had been just a short time earlier. All that day he declined and as night fell it was plain for all to see that young Ruairi lay on his death bed.

'If the dead have life,' Morag cried out, 'I pray that you shall never be a night away from your own bed, my love.'

Ruairi passed away late that night. He had failed so much that his corpse was almost unrecognisable. With great sadness, his remains were taken back over to Rathlin by his family, but in her confinement and grief Morag stayed on Islay. Ruairi was waked and buried among his ancestors on his native island and Morag became a widow before she ever got to see where she was to live.

With everything that had happened, Morag took to her bed, but she slept fitfully. In the middle of the night her dreams were disturbed. In the half light of the glowing peats, she saw her beloved Ruairi coming towards her. He was as hale and hearty as ever he had been.

'My love,' she said, 'is it really you?'

'It is your own true sweetheart,' said Ruairi. 'Wheesht now and listen. You must seek the wise woman. She will know what to do.'

Before Morag could say another word, Ruairi was gone.

In the morning Morag told her mother about the night visit from Ruairi.

'He's in the ground Morag. Didn't they bury him yesterday?'

'I must seek the wise woman,' said Morag, 'I will not rest until I speak with her.'

At last, her mother relented and took her daughter to an old wise woman on the far west of the island.

'Come in girl, come in till I get a look at you. You'll be the one they say is Ruairi the Rathlin lad's widow,' croaked the old woman as Morag entered.

'I'm no widow,' Morag said fiercely, 'My husband is alive. I have seen him.'

'Have you now? Are you sure about that, girl?'

'As sure as I'm standing here,' said Morag defiantly.

Well, to cut a long story short Morag told the wise woman everything that happened and answered all her many strange questions.

'Your man has been taken away by the Lady of the Emerald Isle,' the old woman said eventually.

Most folk don't know who or what the Lady of the Emerald Isle is, and to tell the truth neither did Morag, so the old woman had to put it into plain words for her.

'The Good Folk have been travelling back and forth across the Sea of Moyle from Erin to Alba for generations, sometimes to ceilidh sometimes to quarrel. When they travel together in a band they stir up a whirlwind that can strip the thatch of a roof and lift beasts and even people into the air. That's the faerie wind they call the Lady of the Emerald Isle. Your man was lucky the Good Folk didn't just drop him in the sea, as they're wont to do.'

Morag gasped in horror.

'Have you a brave heart, girl, and a steady hand?' said the old woman, 'For you'll need both. If you falter or fail to follow my instructions to the letter, you'll never see your man again.'

'I will do anything,' said Morag.

'Then listen carefully, girl. You must return to the place where your man was taken up by the Lady of the Emerald Isle. The sooner the better. Bring with you a blade – a reaping hook or a knife. But mind it must be razor sharp and made of iron. Wait until you see an eddy of wind approaching. You must stand your ground no matter how fierce it is. At the very last moment, call out, 'This is for you, give me what is mine.' At the same time, hurl the blade into the heart of the whirlwind with all your strength, and maybe, just maybe, if you've done all I say, your man will be returned to you unharmed. Remember, falter or fail in any particular and you will never see him again.'

Well, that's what Morag did. She stood on the Oa of Islay looking out across the sea, and sure enough didn't a whirlwind soon approach her. It was bigger this time and more powerful. Morag stood her ground until she thought the wind was about to lift her off her feet.

'This is for you, give me what is mine,' she cried and flung a grass hook for all she was worth into the heart of that swirling gusting tower of wind.

No sooner had the hook left her hand, but she fell to the ground and the whirlwind went over her like a herd of stampeding bullocks. From somewhere inside that great eddy of wind Ruairi fell out onto the ground, shaken and dishevelled, but otherwise unharmed. The two young lovers held each other in their arms and wept and laughed and kissed.

'I prayed that you would never be a night away from your own bed, my love,' said Morag breathlessly.

'And your prayers have been answered. You have saved my life,' said Ruairi.

Well, if the wedding festivities on Islay lasted two days and two nights, the ceilidh they had for Ruari's return lasted a week.

But the folk were all wondering who or what was wrapped up in a linen shroud and buried among Ruairi's ancestors on Rathlin Island. With the blessing of the priest, Ruari and his relatives and neighbours gathered in that burying place. The earth that was so sadly shovelled into his grave was once again removed. When they unwrapped the burial shroud it was found to be covering nothing more or less than an old lump of bog oak left in Ruairi's stead by the faerie folk.

Ruairi and then Morag eventually went into that grave on Rathlin, but not for many, many years, for they reared a large family and lived a long and happy life together. Over the years, of course, they often visited Morag's people on Islay, but never again in the month of May when the Lady of the Emerald Isle is most often on the move.

33. Aileen and the Hoodie Crow

This international-type wonder tale was first printed in J.F. Campbell's Popular Tales of the West Highlands, Volume 1 *(Edmonston and Douglas of Edinburgh, 1860). It was collected by Hector MacLean, schoolmaster, from Ann MacGilvray of Islay in April 1859 and was entitled 'The Tale of the Hoodie' (hoodie being a local name for the hooded or grey-backed crow, a common subspecies of the carrion crow). The teller was originally from Cowal on the mainland of Scotland, and she relayed the story in her native Gaelic.*

There is a lot crammed into this story, and for the sake of fluency I have teased out the narrative and reorganised it here and there.

Long, long ago there were three grown-up sisters. All were unmarried and lived with their father. One day they were washing clothes and bathing in a nearby stream when a big grey-backed hoodie crow flew down and landed at the water's edge. Well, all crows are known to be very clever, but even so the young women were greatly surprised when this hoodie spoke.

'Would you marry me, fair maiden?' it said to the oldest sister.

'Marry you? Indeed, I would not,' said she. 'Clever you might be, but you're an ugly brute of a bird.'

The next day the sisters were washing and bathing in the stream once again and back came the big grey-backed hoodie crow.

'Would you marry me, fair maiden?' it said to the middle sister.

'Marry you? Indeed, I would not,' said she. 'Clever you might be, but you're an ugly brute of a bird.'

The next day the sisters were washing and bathing in the stream once more. Back came the big grey-backed hoodie crow.

'Would you marry me, fair maiden?' it said to the youngest sister.

'I would wed you surely, for you are indeed a clever and a handsome bird,' said she without hardly a second thought.

Well, of course this big grey-backed hoodie crow was no ordinary bird. He was a young man under some evil enchantment.

'Would you rather I was a crow by day and your husband by night or your husband by day and a crow by night? he asked his new bride-to-be.

'I would rather you were my husband by day,' she said, 'so that we can be married in God's daylight as woman and man.'

And so that is what happened. The youngest sister, whose name was Aileen, married the strange crow-man. By day he was her loving, handsome husband and everyone remarked on his gleaming jet-black hair with the grey streak running through it. At night he turned back into the hoodie crow and perched at the bottom of her bed with his head under his wing.

Soon after they were wed the crow-man took his young bride to a grand house with servants and maids, and by all accounts there they lived happily in their own strange way. Nine months later Aileen gave birth to a bonnie baby boy and their happiness was complete. That night as they slept, beautiful, otherworldly harp and pipe music was heard drifting through the house and everyone fell into a deep trance. When they awoke in the morning the cradle was empty and the child was nowhere to be found. Aileen and her husband and the entire household were completely brokenhearted.

Time passed – a year and a day – and once again Aileen gave birth to another bonnie baby boy. A watch was kept, but that night the strange, beautiful music was heard once more and again everyone fell into a deep trance. In the morning the child was missing and could not be found. Once again everyone was stricken with grief, and none more so than Aileen.

Time passed – a year and a day – and she gave birth to a third bonnie boy. The guard was doubled in the house and all round about. Aileen's sisters came to help keep a watch, but the same terrible thing happened. Aileen and her husband were inconsolable at the loss of her third baby.

'We must leave this house,' Aileen's husband declared. 'Bring all with you, my love. We can never return to this place for we would rue the day if we did.'

As they went along the road in a coach Aileen suddenly remembered something.

'I have left my wedding ring on the dressing table,' she cried.

In that instant there was a flash of light and a cloud of acrid smoke like the smell of burning hair. Aileen's husband turned into a big grey-backed hoodie crow once more and flew off. Aileen jumped from the coach and ran after her man. When she got to the top of a hill, she could see him down in the next hollow, and when she reached the hollow she could see him soaring over the next high hill, and so it went on all day. Aileen ran over hill and down dale. That evening as dusk fell she came upon a small, lonely cabin and there she begged for some food and shelter.

The woman of the house brought her in. When Aileen saw a little boy playing on the floor, her heart ached for the sons she had lost, and she began to weep. Feeling pity for Aileen, the woman laid her down to rest, but at dawn she awoke with a start and ran out the door. Over hill and down dale she ran in search of her husband, but it was the same again. When she reached the top of a hill she would see a hoodie crow down in the hollow, and when she reached the hollow she would see it soar up over the next high hill.

That evening, exhausted and starving with hunger, Aileen came upon another small cabin. She begged for food and shelter and the woman of the house brought her in. When she saw a little baby boy laughing and gurgling in his cradle, her heart ached for the sons she had lost, and she began to weep. Feeling pity for Aileen, the woman laid

her down to rest, but she awoke at dawn the next morning with a start and without so much as a goodbye, she ran out the door and away.

Over hill and down dale she ran in search of her husband. But alas it was the same again. When she reached the top of a hill she would see a hoodie crow down in the hollow, and when she reached the hollow she would see it soar up over the next hill. All day she chased the crow high up and low down. That evening she was almost dropping off her feet with exhaustion when she came upon a small cabin just like before. Again she begged for food and shelter and the woman of the house brought her in.

When Aileen saw a little baby boy sucking at the woman's breast, her heart ached for the loss of her own sons and, as she wept, she told the woman her tale of woe. When she had finished, the woman felt such sorrow for Aileen.

'This is what you must do,' she said. 'Stay awake all through the night. Your husband might come to you, and that will be your chance get him back. If he comes you must be ready to seize him. No matter what, do not let him go!'

Aileen was wide-eyed with excitement. She tried to stay awake, but so exhausted was she from all her running up hill and down dale that she fell into a fitful sleep. As she tossed and turned, she dreamed that her husband came to her in the form of the hoodie crow. There was something shining in his beak. It was her wedding ring! The crow landed on the bed and slipped the ring onto her finger. As it did, she reached out for the bird and tried to seize it, but it flew off, leaving her with a single black feather in her grasp.

When she awoke in the morning her own gold wedding band was on her finger and in her hand, she held the black feather of a crow.

'What can I do?' she cried. 'I will never see my husband again.'

'All is not lost,' said the woman of the house. 'But to follow your husband, you will have to go through deep forests, climb over mountains of jagged rocks and cross wild bogs. For this you will have to follow the blacksmith's trade and make yourself a set of iron shoes. Remember to make your husband a set if you mean to bring him home.'

And so, Aileen cut off her hair and dressed in men's clothes. She apprenticed herself to a blacksmith for seven long years. There she learned to heat the iron in the forge, strike a hammer blow and send sparks flying off the anvil onto the floor. Only then did she make herself a pair of iron shoes and the same for her husband.

Then she set out on her travels through deep forests, over mountains of jagged rocks and across wild bogs. Eventually she came to a large town in which there was a great air of excitement.

'What is happening here today?' she asked a passerby.

'The biggest wedding we've ever had,' the stranger answered. 'The daughter of the wealthiest man hereabouts is getting married today.'

When the people talked about the strange handsome groom and his gleaming jet-black hair with a grey streak running through it, Aileen knew it was her husband. As the bells rang out and the wedding procession started towards the church, Aileen contrived to somehow get an invitation to the wedding feast, but however she tried she could not. Eventually she tricked her way in and began waiting on the guests, serving their food and drink.

When Aileen came near her husband sitting at the top table, he seemed not to know her. Even when she spoke to him there was not the slightest flicker of memory. As Aileen served him a bowl of broth, she dropped her wedding ring and the black crow feather into it. At the first spoonful he raised the feather in his mouth and with the second the wedding ring.

When the priest stood up to affirm the match the groom bid him to wait.

'Who has put these things in my broth?' he cried.

'It was I. Your true wife and the mother of our three sons,' said Aileen, as she boldly stepped forward for all to see.

There was great intake of breath. It felt as if a spell had been broken – and indeed it was. Aileen took her husband by the hand, and he recognised her. They fled from that place, leaving the bride-to-be and all her wedding guests utterly bewildered.

Wearing the iron shoes Aileen had made, they crossed wild bogs, climbed over mountains of jagged rocks and travelled through deep forests. They ran down dale and over hills. As they came upon each little cottage where Aileen had begged food and shelter, the women of the house handed them back their baby sons one by one. And although many years had passed, the boys were still a little toddler just saying his first few words, an infant not yet walking and a new-born baby.

Eventually Aileen and her husband came back to their grand house with the servants and the maids. Everyone was over-joyed to see them. As far as we know they all lived happily ever after, although it was often said that Aileen's husband could never look at a crow thereafter without a tinge of regret that he would never be able to fly again.

34. The Three Sisters and the Corpse

This story also appears in Campbell's Popular Tales of the West Highlands, *Volume 1, under the title 'The Girl and the Dead Man'. It too was collected by Hector MacLean, but from Islay woman Ann Durroch in May 1858. It follows the pattern of repetition well known as the power or rule of three, which features prominently in many of these international-type wonder tales. In long, drawn-out narratives, it makes it much easier for the storyteller to remember, and emphasises certain motifs.*

For some the more exaggerated and ridiculous the scenarios in these stories, the better. I like this one because the bizarre imagery is not, in my opinion, overplayed.

Long, long ago when folk still told their troubles to the bees, there was a poor woman who had three big grown-up daughters.

'I think, mother,' said the eldest daughter one morning, 'I must go to seek my fortune.'

'I will make ye a bannock then,' said the mother, and she set about preparing the oatmeal and the flour. 'Do you want the best bit and my blessing or the big bit and my curse?' she said when it was baked.

'I would rather have the big bit and your curse,' replied the eldest daughter.

Off she went then, and when she had travelled all day and darkness was falling around her, she sat down by a stone wall to eat her bannock. As she did, the little birds of the woods gathered about.

'Will you give us a few crumbs?' they begged.

'Away you ugly brutes,' cried the eldest daughter. 'I have barely enough for myself.'

'Then our curse on you to go with your mother's,' said the wee birds.

So, when her bannock was eaten, the eldest daughter got up and away she went, and it wasn't half enough to fill her. A bit further along the road she saw a light away in the distance, and if it was a long way off she wasn't long in reaching it. She rapped on the door.

'Who is it?' came the reply in a woman's voice.

'A hard-working maid looking for a good mistress,' said the eldest daughter.

'Just what I am in need of,' the woman said, and let her in. Then the woman revealed that she was the mistress of the household.

'My brother is lying dead in the bed. He is under an enchantment, and I want you to keep a watch on him,' she said. 'Every night you must stay awake and sleep only by day. For this I will pay you a wee peck of gold and the same of silver and, besides, as many hazelnuts as you can crack, as many needles as you can lose, as many thimbles as you can pierce, as much thread as you can use, as many candles as you can burn and a feather bed under ye and an eiderdown for over ye.'

That next night the eldest daughter began her vigil. In the wee hours as she was sewing away, didn't her eyes become heavy? When the mistress found her sleeping, she struck her a blow with a blackthorn stick and the poor girl fell down dead. Then the mistress dragged her outside and threw her on the dung midden behind the house.

Time passed and there was no word of the eldest daughter.

'I think, mother,' said the middle daughter one morning, 'I must follow my sister and go to seek my fortune.'

'I will make ye a bannock then,' said the mother, and she set about preparing the oatmeal and the flour. 'Do you want the best bit and my blessing or the big bit and my curse?' she said when it was baked.

'I would rather have the big bit and your curse,' replied the middle daughter.

Off she went then, and when she had travelled all day and darkness was falling around her, she sat down by the same stone wall to eat her bannock. As she did, the same wee birds of the woods gathered about.

'Will you give us a few crumbs?' they begged.

'Away you ugly brutes,' cried the middle daughter. 'I have barely enough for myself.'

'Then our curse on you to go with your mother's,' said the wee birds once more.

So, when her bannock was eaten, the eldest daughter got up and away she went, and it wasn't half enough to fill her. A bit further along the road she saw a light away in the distance, and if it was a long way off she wasn't long in reaching it. She rapped on the door.

'Who is it?' came the reply in a woman's voice.

'A hard-working maid looking for a good mistress,' said the middle daughter.

'Just what I am looking for,' the woman said, and let her in. The woman then revealed that she was the mistress of the household.

'My brother is lying dead in the bed. He is under an enchantment, and I want you to keep a watch on him,' she said. 'Every night you must stay awake and sleep only by day. For this I will pay you a wee peck of gold and the same of silver and, besides, as many hazelnuts as you can crack, as many needles as you can lose, as many thimbles as you can pierce, as much thread as you can use, as many candles as you can burn and a feather bed under ye and an eiderdown for over ye.'

That next night the middle daughter began her vigil. In the wee hours as she was sewing away, didn't her eyes become heavy? When the mistress found her sleeping, she struck her a blow with a blackthorn stick and the poor girl fell down dead. Then the housewife dragged her outside and threw her on the dung midden behind the house.

Time passed and there was no word of the eldest or the middle daughter.

'I think, mother,' said the youngest daughter one morning, 'I must follow my sisters and go to seek my fortune.'

'I will make ye a bannock then,' said the mother, and she set about preparing the oatmeal and the flour. 'Do you want the best bit and my blessing or the big bit and my curse?' she said when it was baked.

'I would rather have the best bit and your blessing,' replied the youngest daughter.

Off she went then, and when she had travelled all day and darkness was falling around her, she sat down by the same stone wall to eat her bannock. As she did, the same wee birds of the woods gathered about again.

'Will you give us a few crumbs?' they said.

'Of course I will,' cried the youngest daughter. 'I have plenty enough food for us all.'

'Then a blessing on you to go with your mother's,' said the wee birds.

So up the youngest daughter got and away she went when her bannock was only half eaten, and it was more than enough to fill her. A bit further along the road she saw a light away in the distance, and if it was a long way off she wasn't long in reaching it. She rapped on the door.

'Who is it?' came the reply in a woman's voice.

'A hard-working maid looking for a good mistress,' said the youngest daughter.

'Just what I am looking for,' the woman said, and let her in. The woman then revealed that she was the mistress of the household.

'My brother is lying dead in the bed. He is under an enchantment, and I want you to keep a watch on him,' she said. 'Every night you must stay awake and sleep only by day. For this I will pay you a wee peck of gold and the same of silver and, besides, as many hazelnuts as you can crack, as many needles as you can lose, as many thimbles as you can pierce, as much thread as you can use, as many candles as you can burn and a feather bed under ye and an eiderdown for over ye.'

That next night the youngest daughter began her vigil. In the wee hours as she was sewing away, didn't the corpse begin to rise?

'Lie down or I will give you a good leathering with this blackthorn stick,' said the youngest daughter sternly.

Well, the corpse lay down peacefully and the youngest daughter kept on with her vigil and her sewing. A while later, the corpse rose again and this time grinned foolishly at the youngest daughter. Again, she gave it fair warning and it lay down peacefully.

When the corpse rose for the third time, she gave it a belt with the blackthorn stick and was about to do so again, but the corpse took a hold of the other end and wouldn't let go. A tug-of-war ensued, and back and forward they went either end of the stick. They ended up outside, back and forward and through the woods. The hazelnuts were knocking the eyes out of them and the thorns tearing the ears off them. Eventually they got back to the house and by now the corpse was fully revived. The colour came back into his cheeks and the dead brother was alive as you or me.

The youngest daughter got paid her wages – a wee peck of gold and the same of silver – and besides the woman gave her a tonic corked in a bottle and told her where to find her sisters. She went out to the midden and trickled the tonic onto their lips and what do you know? It brought them both back to life!

The three sisters all returned home to their mother's house and if they lived happily ever after I'm happy for them, and if they did not – well then, just let them be.

CARA

35. The Cara Brownie

I have already covered the general nature of brownies in my introduction to 'The Brownie of Baugh'. The Cara Brownie is not a different creature, but is of an altogether more meticulous and impish disposition. Just like humans, brownies have different personalities and while always helpful, some are more amiable than others. The Cara Brownie is more characterful than most and is much more to my liking.

The tiny island of Cara lies less than half a mile south of its nearest neighbour, Gigha. It is said to be the only island left in the Hebrides that is still in the possession of the McDonnell (McDonald) Clan, who can trace their lineage to the Lords of the Isles. Only one inhabitable dwelling remains: Cara House, home of the McDonalds of Largie. At the southern tip of the islet is a rocky outcrop called the Mull of Cara. On the grassy slope below there is a block of stone that since time out of memory has been known as the Brownie's Chair. It is said that visitors to the island would do well to pay their respects to the Brownie of Cara, less they should fall foul of him.

The main ingredients for this tale came from McGregor's The Peat Fire Flame, *though the Cara Brownie also features in various tourist information brochures and online articles, which were helpful.*

The Cara Brownie once resided in the old Castle of Largie. It was the home of his master, the McDonald of Largie, and was situated above the shore on the western side of the Mull of Kintyre. When the McDonalds deserted Largie Castle for the Isle of Cara, the brownie flitted with the rest of the household to take up residence in Cara House. There he continued his old duties as guardian of the McDonald family and their fortunes.

He was faithful, of course, and bore an abiding ill will to the McDonalds' most despised enemy – the Campbells. At the mere mention of their name, he would smash some glass or crockery. That said, he was no grovelling servant. He did not suffer any idle or foul behaviour from family member or guest and was wont to chastise them just as he pleased.

Like others of his kind, he lived largely, if not entirely, on milk and cream, which was left for him at a certain place every evening before the household retired for the night. In return, and without having to be told, the Cara Brownie made all the necessary preparations for the arrival of guests and unexpected strangers. He aired the rooms and beds and changed the bedclothes when necessary. Without fail, he made sure that no unclean earthenware, plates or cutlery were left for the maids in the morning. Dirty linen was washed and left to dry, and at night all the dogs were quietly removed to be kennelled outdoors. In short, the Cara Brownie kept the house like a palace and her home fires burning. No chieftain's residence was better managed and maintained than Cara House.

Fastidious as he was, the Cara Brownie could not abide slovenliness in family members or guests. Those who wantonly left flagons and tumblers lying around with their contents spilling onto the stone flags were often rudely awakened by the sudden sound of breaking stoneware or by a sharp skelp (slap) around the ear, administered in the dark by the invisible hand of the Cara Brownie.

That he did not suffer fools gladly and had no patience for drunkards was well known by the household and soon grasped by intemperate visitors. On more than one occasion drunken revellers who had taken to bed, and were snoring loudly, awoke to find themselves stark naked before a mouldering fire or, worse still, outside in the cold night air.

One time a milk maid charged with bringing the cows home was waylaid by an amorous young farmhand. When she lost track of the time and the beasts in her care, she ran for home in sheer panic only to find the animals all tied up in their stalls contentedly chewing on their cuds.

The McDonalds of Largie could never have asked or paid for a better housekeeper, but alas the old house was deemed to be in bad need of repairs and renovation and, eventually, replacement. This, it seems, was too much for the Cara Brownie. He left off his cleaning and catering, and since long many a year has never made his presence felt. I suppose the McDonalds would have him back in a heartbeat, but everyone knows a brownie, once offended, never returns to his former duties and thereafter refuses all bribes and offers of milk and cream.

ARGYLL AND KINTYRE

36. Robin óg and the Faerie Pipes

Throughout the Kingdom of Dál Riada, there has long been a fervent belief in the existence of the faeries. Over the years many stories have been told by people who claimed to have had encounters of one kind or another with the wee folk. Whole volumes have been dedicated to describing them and unearthing the mysteries of their otherworldly natures (see sources).

In his book The Peat Fire Flame, *McGregor relates two reports from the Isle of Muck in which spellbound children claim to have seen and talked to the faeries, and another about a young man who heard their music. Accounts of this kind were once common, and even in the twenty-first century I have spoken to old people in the Glens of Antrim who quite sincerely claim to have had encounters with faerie folk in their youth.*

There was once a young man by the name of Robin óg – young Robin. His people came from Argyll but their family name has long since been forgotten. When passing a faerie mound of an evening, he would always stop and, gently creeping onto it, put his ear to the ground to listen for the faerie music. The jigs and reels were like no others he had ever heard. They were full of wild runs and such playful and delicate ornamentation.

Many a time Robin óg wished that he could play his pipes half as well. If he could, he dreamed, then he would be called upon to play at every ceilidh and every wedding and every funeral in the country. Never would he want for food or drink, or a soft bed for the night, or a charming young lassie to catch his eye. He might even be called upon to play for the clan chief or even the king. His name would be known throughout the land – Robin óg of the Pipes.

One night his longing sent him tiptoeing to the door of a wise woman to seek counsel on the matter.

'I want to be able to play like the faerie pipers,' he told the old woman.

'The faerie music is not for the likes of you,' said she.

'Please. Help me,' he begged. 'I have learned all their tunes in my head, but I cannot find the notes on my chanter.'

The old woman laughed. 'It's a set of faerie pipes you're after, then.'

'Yes. I think so. Maybe,' faltered Robin óg.

'This is what you must do then,' said the old woman. 'Go to the faerie mound and onto it throw something of value to you. Say the words, "This is mine, give me what is yours", and you will see what you will see.'

The next evening Robin óg went to the earthen mound and crept closer nervously. He had not given much thought as to what he might be willing to part with. He was very poor and did not possess many things, and certainly nothing of any great value like silver or gold. But then he took the bonnet from his head and looked at it. It had been knitted by his mother years before, and though it was tattered and torn Robin óg loved it and, under any other circumstances, he would not have parted with it for the world.

Suddenly he tossed his beloved bonnet through the air. It landed on the faerie mound, and he called out, 'This is mine, give me what is yours.' The moment the words left his mouth, a set of pipes about a quarter the size of his own appeared on the ground before him. They were perfect in every detail. They were turned from some black hardwood and mounted with silver ferrules. The wee bag was of the softest leather and stitched with the finest waxed thread. When Robin óg filled the bag and blew into the chanter the sweetest, most magical music filled the night air. Like a child, he was fit to burst with sheer delight.

Robin óg stowed the pipes inside his coat and ran home to tell his mother and play for her the faerie music. When he got home his mother sat by the peat fire wide-eyed as her son regaled her with every detail of his story. When he put his hand inside his coat to fetch out the set of faerie pipes all that he found was a dusty old puffball and a few crumpled lengths of hollow reed.

Robin óg gained nothing from his brief sally with the faerie folk. Few if any ever do. Often it was he lamented the loss of his much-loved bonnet and cursed his own foolishness. They say he never played the pipes again, not at ceilidhs nor weddings, funerals or anywhere. And that is why his family name has long since been forgotten.

37. Black McKenzie of the Pipes

Versions of the following tale are widespread throughout Dál Riada and far beyond. In fact, wherever there is a faerie hill to be found a version of this tale will be told, usually varying only in small details of the local surroundings. This account is a slightly darker than usual, and for that reason alone it deserves inclusion here.

It is based mainly on a rendering found in McGregor's The Peat Fire Flame, *but also a few other sources.*

There was another young fellow one time by the name of Black McKenzie — on account of his wild mane of black hair — who lived on the shore of Loch Linnhe, south of Barcaldine. He was a weaver by trade, but like many young men he enjoyed a tune on the pipes and a wee dram of whiskey to help the music along.

One night McKenzie and a friend were merrily wending their way home from a ceilidh somewhere. On McKenzie's shoulder rode a stone jar half full of good whisky. Their journey homewards took them past a little hill well known to be a faerie mound. As they glanced toward it they could see an opening with light shining from it and the strains of music and revelry streaming out into the night. With the excitement and joy of their own ceilidh still on them and the whisky filling them with courage, the two young fellows crept closer to the faerie mound.

Inside they could see faerie pipers tearing away, and the music they were playing was heady and enchanting. There were other faeries spinning about and dancing and having a grand old time. Without thinking a thing about it, McKenzie entered, so entranced was he by the music and antics of the wee faerie folk. His friend followed, but he had the presence of mind to stick a knife into the door jamb.

Soon McKenzie was dancing like a man possessed. Reel after jig after reel he danced with the wee folk and never seemed to tire. His friend pleaded with him to slow down and later to depart, but McKenzie paid not the slightest bit of heed. Eventually his friend could wait no longer. He left McKenzie to his dancing and staggered home alone.

The following day the friend had to explain to McKenzie's parents the strange circumstances surrounding the disappearance of their son. They were disbelieving at first and suspected foul play. Nevertheless, it was decided that if their son did not return by the end of a year, they would risk the wrath of the faeries. In the hope of finding him dead or alive, they would dig down into the faerie mound from above.

A year passed and still there was no sign of McKenzie. And so, a year and a day after he disappeared so mysteriously, his friends and relatives gathered and nervously they began to dig down into the earth where lived the faeries. There they found McKenzie still dancing like a madman to the wild otherworldly music.

Of course, the faeries were raging mad at this intrusion and daggers were drawn. Only by good fortune and some very quick thinking on the part of McKenzie's people was a fearful altercation avoided. To cut a long story short, McKenzie was rescued, though at first he was vexed that his night's fun had been so rudely interrupted. It took a long time to convince him he had been 'away with the faeries' for a year and a day. Once back in the land of the living, it was seen that McKenzie was a shadow of the sturdy young man he had been. For another year he was unable to work, so weak and failed had he become.

As time passed, however, he regained much of his strength. The first day he sat down to weave his shuttle flew with great speed, and the folk said of him that he had gained the 'faerie shuttle'. From then on he could weave three times as much cloth as any mortal weaver. The Laird of Barcaldine promoted him to weaver-in-chief and his fame grew throughout the countryside.

But McKenzie could never get those faerie tunes out of his head. Always he was haunted and always he tried to play them on his pipes. Never satisfied with what he heard, he began to fashion his own pipes to see if he could make any improvement. His fame as a piper and maker of pipes spread further than his fame as a weaver and he soon became known as Black McKenzie of the Pipes.

But even though McKenzie's weaving and piping improved greatly after his time with the faeries, he never enjoyed a day's good health or true happiness again. They say he died a restless and discontented man long before his time.

38. The Chieftain, the Crane and the Cook

*The common crane (*Grus grus*) has recently made a return to Ireland as a breeding bird, having been absent for over 300 years. Standing 4ft tall with a 7ft wingspan, it was once widespread, and it appears in ancient Irish myths and legends too numerous to mention here. The word crane here, however, may simply be a misnomer for the grey heron (*Ardea cinerea*).*

This delightful little story is from the vast repertoire of the renowned Scottish traveller and storyteller Duncan Williamson, who heard it as a child from his father. It appears in The Genie and the Fisherman, *by Duncan and Linda Williamson (Cambridge University Press, 1991), under the title 'The Laird and the Crane'. It may be more of an international tale than one firmly rooted in the traditions of Dál Riada, but I couldn't resist its charm.*

Duncan Williamson told it as a children's story but, with the kind permission of his widow, Linda, I have developed a slightly more adult version. I include it here on the grounds that Williamson spent much of his youth on the west coast and many of his stories come from or are set in this part of the world.

To celebrate high days and holidays, the people of Dál Riada used to feast on venison and wild boar, but also on delicacies such as ducks and geese. Swans were always revered and never eaten by humble folk. But in those far off days big, long-legged, long-necked cranes were a common enough sight on marshlands and peatbogs. They were long considered to be the finest eating fowl of them all – little wonder they are so rare now!

Anyway, one time this proud old chieftain decided he would have a great feast and invite all his clansmen and neighbours. He ordered that a crane should be killed, and then he sent for his most trusted servant – the cook.

'I want you to roast the crane, and when everyone is assembled bring it out on a covered platter and set it down in front of me. I will carve it myself and portion out the meat.'

'Very good my lord,' said the cook.

The day of the great feast arrived, and the cook began to roast all the meats and bake the breads. He had made sure the household was well stocked with mead and ale and, of course, he had to sample them. As he worked away by the heat of the kitchen fires preparing the banquet, he helped himself to an odd wee nip of mead or a tumbler full of ale.

As the day wore on, didn't he slowly fall under the influence of the liquor? And by the time he had the crane roasted and he was lifting it off the spit, wasn't his belly fair rumbling, and a fierce hunger was on him? Of course, well he knew how tasty the flesh of the crane would be. His mouth was watering that much his teeth were nearly floating, and he began smacking his lips like a pig about to be fed.

'Sure, his lordship won't miss one wee bit of the crane,' he said to himself, and didn't he pull a drumstick off and sink his teeth into the juicy delicious meat? Oh, it just melted in his mouth it was that tender. When he ate that he couldn't help himself but pull the thigh off too, and it was even tastier.

Well, the whole leg of the crane was a brave feed and that done him. He covered up the bird, for he didn't like to look at it now with one leg missing.

Now that the hunger was off him, the cook began to fret. 'What will I do at all?' he said to himself, 'His lordship will have my head for this.'

When all the guests were seated and their cups and tumblers charged with liquor, the old chieftain signed for the crane to be brought out and the cook carried it from the kitchen on a covered platter. He could hardly contain himself with excitement, but when he lifted the lid off the platter his eyes went straight to where the missing leg should have been. Immediately he slammed the lid back in place.

'Take this away,' he roared at the cook. 'You have disgraced me in front of my guests. I will deal with you later.'

Well, the feasting went on to a very late hour, but the old chieftain was fuming. He couldn't wait for his guests to leave so he could challenge the cook. For his part, the cook was agonising about what he was going say, for he knew he would have to answer for himself sooner or later. The minute the last guest left he was sent for.

'Explain yourself to me, and mind your head is in the balance,' said the chieftain sternly.

'Explain myself my lord? What do you mean?' replied the cook as innocently as a child.

'Tell me this instant why the crane had only one leg.'

'Sure, all cranes only have one leg my lord,' said the cook straight back to his master.

'Don't insult me or I will strike your head off this very moment.'

'Forgive me, my lord, I don't mean to insult you, but all the cranes I have ever seen only had the one leg.'

Well, the difference of opinion went back and forth a few times but eventually the old chieftain had enough.

'Put this man in irons,' he roared, 'Tomorrow we will go out at dawn in search of a crane. If it is found to have only one leg then your head will be spared, but if not …'

Sure, enough the next morning dawned clear and bright, and the place was white with frost. Out went the old chieftain with his men and the cook still bound in irons. Soon they came to a wild misty place where the cranes dwelled. When they came near a solitary bird, wasn't it standing on one leg?

'There you are my lord. Didn't I tell you – cranes only have the one leg.'

At that moment the old chieftain clapped his hands. The crane's other leg appeared, and the bird took flight.

'Prepare your soul for eternity,' said the chieftain. 'Have you anything you wish to say before you lose your head?'

'Just one thing my lord.'

'Very well, speak it now.'

'Well, my lord maybe if you had clapped your hands at the table last evening that crane would have put down its other leg and all this fuss could have been avoided.'

Well, this made the old chieftain smile, and when he laughed so everyone else did. Their mirth and laughter brought great relief to the poor cook.

'You are as wily as an old fox,' said the chieftain. 'Your wit has saved you yet again.'

There and then he ordered the cook to be released and afterwards he said that he never really intended to take the head of his most trusted servant.

The cook was not so certain, however, and never again did he risk serving up a one-legged fowl to his master. At feasts on high days and holy days for many years after, the old chieftain delighted his guests – not with the flesh of a roasted crane – but with the story I have just told you.

39. The Kintyre Fox

Foxes have long been considered very clever by country folk. They have also had other, less complimentary, attributes like slyness and wantonness projected on to them by those who misinterpret the fox's natural survival strategies. Stories abound throughout Europe about Reynard the trickster fox who outwits farmers, shepherds and other creatures. In other cultures around the world foxes are similarly portrayed. In this tale the fox is exceptionally clever. Even so, the young Mull of Kintyre shepherd proves to be more than a match.

Notoriously, foxes are the bane of sheep farmers – however, there is growing evidence that they usually only take dead or dying lambs, a fact reasonably well documented by research scientists (see Running with the Fox, *David MacDonald, Unwin Hyman, 1987).*

I found the makings of this story in McGregor's The Peat Fire Flame *(see also foreword by Dr David Hume MBE with reference to the story of Todd Rodden).*

Once, a very long time ago when wild boar and wolves still wandered the countryside, there lived a fox on the west coast of the Mull of Kintyre. It was said he was so clever that to forestall undue attention he never took fur nor feather within 20 miles of his den.

When he did go raiding the sheepfolds of Kintyre, the shepherds' dogs would always give chase. All through the heather and woods they tracked his scent, but never could they catch him. When the shepherds went to investigate they would find one or two of their hounds lying dead at the bottom of a deep gorge. The only explanation was that the cruel fox led his pursuers to that place and leapt across the gorge. In the heat of the chase the poor hounds were lured to their deaths.

How the fox was able to find a footing on the opposite side of the gorge no one could understand, for on the sheer rock face there was neither a ledge nor a lip big enough for the claw of a squirrel nor even a wee bird to land. For years the shepherds all around that locality wondered at the cleverness of the Kintyre fox and lamented the loss of their hounds.

One day the shepherds set out for the gorge with a rope and a young shepherd lad who was light enough and brave enough to be lowered into its depths. Down he went on the end of the rope, carefully peering into every crack and crevice. A few feet down he came upon some ash saplings growing out of the rock and straining up towards the light of day. One was about the thickness of his thumb and more supple than the rest. It had, scored into its bark near the end, strange marks as if it had been gnawed. When the lad placed his weight upon it he discovered that it bent across the gorge easily enough to bridge the gap and come with touching distance of a convenient ledge on the other side.

Soon pictures began to form in the young fellow's mind, where the clever fox leapt down into the gorge and, trusting his own natural agility, grabbed hold of the sapling with his teeth. His weight and momentum were enough to bend the sapling sufficiently that he could find his footing on the ledge

opposite and, from there, scramble up to the top of the gorge. 'It's pure animal genius,' thought the young lad, but it was also as far-fetched as faerie's gold.

Nevertheless, the shepherd lad took out a knife and began to cut through the ash tree at its base. On second thoughts, he left the sapling where it was but cut part way through. 'If you're half as clever as I think ye are, my wee red friend,' said the young shepherd to himself, 'then the next time ye come a raiding ye'll meet your maker at the bottom o' this gully.'

Sure enough, the next time the fox came around the sheep folds, didn't the hounds give chase? All through the heather and woods they tracked his scent. When the shepherds went to see, didn't they find the fox lying dead at the bottom of the gorge, the broken sapling clenched in his teeth?

For years after, the folk round about told the story of the Kintyre Fox. Of course, it was always meant as a cautionary tale against the dangers of being too clever or overconfident for, clever and all as the Kintyre Fox thought he was, didn't a young shepherd lad outwit him?

Even so, the shepherd lad's name has long been forgotten, but the Kintyre Fox is still remembered as the hero of the story. And still in that part of the country, anyone showing great quickness of mind or daring is said to be as clever as the Kintyre Fox. To this day, that gorge on the west coast of the Mull of Kintyre is still known as Carraig an tSionnaich – the Rock of the Fox.

40. Caivala of the Glossy Hair

This story was first published in J.P. MacLean's History of the Clan McClean *(Robert Clarke & Co., Cincinnati, 1889) but also appears in* West Highland Tales *by Fitzroy MacLean. Family records show that Iain Mor Tanister MacDonald (d. 1427) married Majory Bisset (d. 1419), daughter of John the Good, who was Lord of the Antrim Glynns (see* The Antrim McDonnells, *Angela Antrim, Ulster Television Production, 1977). This fact would later be called upon as the foundation for the infamous Sorley Boy MacDonnell's claim to that title. One of their descendants is Randal McDonnell, 15th Earl of Antrim and the current occupant of the family seat at Glenarm Castle.*

Straying a little from historical facts, this story bears strong similarities to that of Maeve Roe – whose ghost is said to haunt Dunluce Castle – and her lover, Reginald O'Cahan, who suffered a worse fate to the protagonists here (see Haunted Antrim, *Madeline McCully, The History Press, 2017).*

Iain Mor MacDonald of Kintyre was the younger brother of Donald, Second Lord of the Isles. Having less weight on his shoulders, he was free to follow his heart's desire and sail across the Sea of Moyle to hunt in the Antrim Hills. One day he came across a huge Irish warrior coming down a narrow glen. He was mounted on a horse, and behind was a beautiful glossy-haired maiden. She was weeping and wailing loudly, and seeing this MacDonald held up the warrior.

'What troubles the girl?' he asked the Irishman.

'None of your business, unless you want the same as her da got,' said he fiercely.

To shorten the story, the warrior, whose name was O'Doherty, had left the maiden's father, who was the Earl of the Antrim Glens, for dead nearby and carried off his daughter, Caivala of the Glossy Hair, who was now, understandably, in such distress.

By the time MacDonald realised this, O'Doherty had already dismounted and drawn his sword. The two then clashed and fought bitterly to the death. It was MacDonald who slew O'Doherty, although he was severely wounded in the fight.

With what was left of his strength, and helped by Caivala of the Glossy Hair, McDonald carried the Earl of Antrim back to his stronghold on the coast of Antrim. There the two men recovered from their injuries. While under the protection of the Earl of Antrim, MacDonald spent many happy hours with his daughter, singing and dallying with one another. When it came time for him to return to Alba, he asked to speak with the Earl alone.

'I beg your permission,' said he, 'to marry your daughter.'

'I do not give it,' cried the old chieftain. 'My daughter can trace her kin back to the High Kings of Ireland. You insult my ancestry.'

'I am Iain Mor MacDonald, Lord of Kintyre and brother to the Lord of the Isles and King of the Hebrides.'

His claim was to no avail. Iain Mor tried to convince the Earl that a marriage between the two families would be advantageous to both, but a fierce row broke out between the two men. In the end, the Earl took the upper hand. He summoned men and Iain Mor was easily overpowered.

That night as MacDonald lay in his cold chamber awaiting what fate lay ahead, he heard the locks being undone and the door opening. Before he moved to defend himself, he realised it was Caivala come to rescue him.

'You must flee, my love,' she said, 'before my father's temper leads us to ruin.'

Not long after this, Iain Mor was back on the shore of Kintyre. When news reached him that the Earl had confined his own daughter for refusing to marry any of the suitors he brought forth, MacDonald had no choice but return to Erin. This time he did not speak with the Earl, but between them the two lovers contrived to free Caivala and made good their escape.

Within days they were wed and, though the Earl of Antrim cursed and threatened, the couple remained steadfast. In time the Earl's displeasure waned, and he relented. He invited his daughter and son-in-law over to Antrim and greeted them most hospitably. The two men made a pact of friendship between their clans that proved lasting and strong.

The years went by, and the old Earl of Antrim died. His title and deeds passed to Iain Mor MacDonald, Lord of Kintyre and the MacDonalds, or as they came to be, the McDonnells. This line of the family have been the Earls of Antrim ever since.

RATHLIN

41. The Strange Guests

This unusual little Rathlin story appears as a very brief sketch in Lady Wilde's Ancient Legends, Mystic Charms and Superstitions of Ireland *(Ward and Downey, London, 1888). It seems to turn the table on the image of islanders, who are much more often portrayed in folk tales and history as victims of the merciless onslaught of various waves of invaders – rival clansmen, Viking raiders and English tyrant overlords. It is all the more interesting for that.*

Sadly, Wilde gives no information as to how or from whom the story was taken down. It was probably a well-known tale on the island once, though I have not come across it either as a Rathlin story or otherwise.

For centuries seafaring men had come to Rathlin Island to seek sanctuary from their enemies, shelter from the weather or to plunder the island's riches such as they were. For the islanders this was an everyday reality of their hard existence. The arrival of visitors could be a blessing, but was more often a curse. The islanders were not always passive creatures subject to the whims of unwanted guests, however. Yes, they were often raided and robbed, but they could defend themselves too, and sometimes they became the aggressors and the plunderers.

So it was one time when a longship appeared on the horizon and strangers stepped ashore. Although they bore arms and looked like warriors who had campaigned hard in distant battles, they were civil enough to ask for food and shelter in return for payment.

The islanders welcomed them well enough. A bullock was slaughtered and butchered, and a great feast was prepared in honour of their guests.

'Bring no weapons to the table for you will not need them here,' the visitors were told, but the islanders secretly planned a bloody massacre. When the ale flowed freely, and their visitors had eaten and drunk their fill, it was then the islanders intended to carry out their cruel plan. Throats would be cut and men slain as they slept. It would not be an honourable fight, if there were such a thing. The island-ers' only end was to rob their victims of their valuables and dump what was left in the sea for the fishes to feed on.

When the visitors came to the feasting tables, each man drew his long knife, and with great purpose stuck the blade into the timber boards in front of him. At that moment the islanders realised that somehow their murderous plan had been discovered. All boldness and conviction evaporated like the dew on a summer's morning. The islanders made no attempt to act. An uneasy meal followed, but the strange visitors accepted all kindnesses as if they were offered sincerely. They made every effort to be courteous and not the slightest insult was given to their hosts.

All night the seemingly jovial feasting went on. Eventually the islanders were lulled off to sleep where they sat with songs and stories of strange lands and heroic deeds. When they stirred late in the morning they discovered their visitors had left without so much as an angry word. It was a great relief to the islanders that no blood had been spilled – not least their own. Where each warrior had been seated the night before a gold coin was placed to cover the hole that his knife blade had left in the wooden tables. All told it was a princely sum and a generous recompense for such treacherous hospitality.

The islanders were shamed and repentant. They made a promise to themselves to offer a warm and genuine welcome to their kindly visitors if ever they came back. For a long time, the islanders watched the horizon in hope, but the strangers never returned.

It was always said that ever after the people of Rathlin Island were very helpful and hospitable to wayfarers who chanced to land upon their shore. This was many years ago and untold visitors have come and gone. Doubtless some have been more welcome than others. Whether the promise is kept still, only the visitor of today can judge.

42. The Sleeping Warriors

Robert the Bruce, erstwhile king of Scotland, had strong connections with the north-east of Ireland. Very famously, he fled Scotland with 300 of his loyal supporters in 1306 and sought sanctuary on Rathlin Island. It was in what became known as 'Bruce's Cave' (not to be confused with Bruce's Castle) while watching the spider that he was said to have had his great moment of inspiration before returning to Scotland to claim the crown – but that is another story!

The motif of the sleeping king or chief with his retinue of slumbering warriors awaiting the call to defend their nation in some future time of need is an old and common one found in many folk tales and myths across Europe. In Ireland and Scotland, of course, it is usually Fionn mac Cumhaill and the men of the Fiana who are thus portrayed. Other famous characters similarly dormant and awaiting the call include King Arthur and Ogier the Dane. Not surprising, then, that a historic figure like Robert the Bruce was similarly enshrined.

The basic ingredients of the following tale also appear in Lady Wilde's Ancient Legends, Mystic Charms and Superstitions of Ireland *under the title 'Rathlin Island'.*

It was told on Rathlin that beneath the ruins of Bruce's Castle is a great cavern, the entrance to which is only revealed once every seven years for a few fleeting hours. Inside, so the legend says, sleep Robert the Bruce and his men, who are dreaming of the day they will rise up and dispossess Ireland of Rathlin Island and restore her once more to the sovereignty of Scotland. How this came to be known was through the first-hand account of one young island man whose name has, alas, been long forgotten.

He had been fishing underneath Bruce's Castle when he noticed an opening that he had never before seen. Greatly intrigued, he went closer and ventured inside. The air was still and rank. He could hear what sounded like the heavy breathing and snoring and breaking of wind of an army of men at rest, which made his hair stand on end. Trying to convince himself it was just the sounds of the restless sea coming and going through crevices and crannies deep in the rock, he went further inside the cave.

When his eyes adjusted to the dim light, the island man eventually saw, to his utter amazement, that indeed there was an army of men encamped there, and every one of them fast asleep. Each was dressed in chain mail and studded leather breast plates and the like, and by each warrior's side lay a claidheamh mòr (claymore), a mighty battle axe or a pike. In the middle of them all a great chieftain reclined, and on his head he wore the crown of kingship. It was none other than Robert the Bruce himself and no mistake, for on his outer shirt was emblazoned in red and gold the emblem of a rampant lion. Other royal standards and banners hung limp where they rested against walls nearby.

The man shook in great fear, but a greater excitement urged him on, for he wanted proof of all he was witness to.

Tiptoeing through the tangle of slumbering bodies and weaponry, he found a claidheamh mòr half unsheathed. As gently as he could, he lifted the great sword by the hilt – 6ft long and weighing as much as a fat goose. The moment he did so the warriors began to stir.

'Who is it dares to enter the chamber of the great Bruce?' bellowed one of the warriors as he rubbed the sleep from his eyes.

'Is it time?' asked another, yawning and stretching his ancient limbs.

The island man dropped the sword with a clatter and clang and ran for his life. He could hear oaths and curses being hurled after him. Just as he came out into the daylight, there was a tremor and a roar like thunder. The ground shook under his feet and when he peered over his shoulder he saw that the opening of the cavern had closed.

That the island man had laid eyes on Robert the Bruce and his army not a single person ever doubted. Hadn't he described every trifling detail of what he had seen, right down to the warriors' unkempt hair and their tatty beards? He even remarked that they smelled worse than a herd of buck goats. All this he swore to on his unborn children's graves, and sure, what good would it do a man to make up such a story?

43. The White Horse – An Capall Bán

Of course, there are many stories that feature white horses, and they are popular in the folklore of many cultures far beyond the shores of Dál Riada, especially, and for obvious reasons, those with maritime connections.

The motif of an enchanted island, as noted elsewhere, is also both common and widespread. It seems, perhaps unsurprisingly, particularly well loved in the folklore of Rathlin Island. This beautiful and poignant Rathlin folk tale, however, is quite an unusual version of the premise.

The following was adapted from a rendering found in Augustine McCurdy's Stories and Legends of Rathlin *(self-published, 2006) and other sources.*

It was many long years ago on a wild and stormy night that, in a lonely cabin on Rathlin where lived an old woman, a knock came to the door.

'Come in, whoever ye are,' called the woman, not expecting any visitors on such a night but thinking now that it would be one of her island neighbours in need of something. The latch lifted on the door and in from the wind and rain came a young man. He was a stranger to the old woman.

'Sorry to disturb ye on such a night as this and it so late but I saw your light from down by the shore and followed it,' said the stranger.

'You're welcome, young fella. Come in now and take off your coat, for I'm sure you're ringing wet,' said she, not thinking anything untoward. However, as she spoke the words she noticed that his cloak was as dry as snuff.

'Thank you,' said the stranger. 'Would you have anywhere I could put my head down for the night?'

The old woman directed him to a settle bed by the fire and got up to make a drop of *tae* and a bite of meat. As she worked she enquired, by way of conversation, how the young man had come, for she knew no island boats would have been out in such foul weather.

'I did not come by boat,' said the young man, but he offered no further explanation as to how he had arrived on the island. 'I am here in search of my father. He set out for Rathlin many years ago, but since then I have had no word of him. Often it was he told me we had relatives around these shores, and I would dearly like to make their acquaintance.'

'I see,' said the woman as she poured out the *tae* and they ate their bread and butter in silence. Eventually the woman ventured to speak again.

'When I was a little girl,' she said, 'I remember my mother telling me about a strange man who, not unlike yourself sir, appeared on the island one stormy night. She said he went about asking people after an ancestor who had been a Rathlin seafarer many years before. When the people heard the name, the older ones remembered him. They told him that they had heard his ship was lost with all hands and that there was none of his connection left on the island. The islanders all remarked to one another that the stranger was very mysterious. No one could understand how he had managed to land on the island, for he had no boat himself, and no one had brought him.

'Anyway, they kept a watch and followed him about the island until he went down to a place called Bernes Cave. He stood there for a long time staring out to sea, and then he uttered an unearthly cry as if in agony. Just then a great white stallion rose up out of the sea and the man leapt onto its back. Rider and horse galloped off with great speed away into the raging, foaming waters towards the western ocean and were seen no more. If not for many folk seeing this with their own eyes, it would not have been believed.'

The young man listened to the story without saying a word. At length he spoke.

'The man you speak of is my father,' he said with a long sigh. 'Now there is nothing here for me. I must away at dawn, but I am weary and in need of rest.'

With that the old woman bid her guest goodnight. When she arose just a few hours later she stoked the fire and heated some porridge for the young man's breakfast.

'Tell me,' she said, 'from what part of the world do you come?'

'You have been kind to me,' said the young man, 'so I will tell you about my land – the Blessed Isle – and it's there I will soon return to. It lies far out in the western ocean, many days' sailing from Rathlin. It is bound all around by high golden cliffs and has only one safe place to anchor. The weather is always fine, and the land verdant and plentiful. No one ever grows old where I come from.

'Many ships have sailed past my island home and not even known of its existence, for it is only briefly visible to the mortal eye once in every seven years. The men of those few ships who have happened upon my island are always entranced. If they come ashore they are always warned that if they do not depart with the next tide then they are bound to stay forevermore. Few ever leave or want to. Those who leave become mortal once again and for every year they have spent on the Blessed Isle a hundred years fall upon them. And now I must return to my home. Come with me, if you wish.'

'I thank you,' said the old woman, 'but I wish to die here on my own island.'

'Very well,' said the young man, and with that he took his leave.

The old woman followed him at a distance, and as she walked along she met other islanders to whom she quickly whispered the story, and they also came to witness the stranger's leaving. Down to Bernes Cave he went and, as his father had done before him, he stood there staring at the ocean for a long time. Then he called up his white stallion with the same unearthly cry. He leapt onto the animal's back and galloped off toward the western ocean.

A great sadness fell over the people as they watched him fade into the far distance. They had a great many questions they would have liked to ask him about friends and family who had been lost at sea, but now their chance was gone forever.

44. The Fisherman and his Wife

This story is developed from a very fragmented sketch found in the National Folklore Collection, Main Collection, under the title, 'A Folktale from Rathlin, 1920 (ATO555: The Fisher and his Wife)'. It was recorded from an old man named Séamus McFaul by SOD' (Séamus Ó Duilearga). The original manuscript is written in Rathlin Irish, which is more akin to Scots Gaelic, and the dialect quite distinct even from Ulster Gaelic. Despite all efforts to translate by Co. Antrim Irish language scholar Brian McLaughlan, it was clearly incomplete. This probably indicates that the teller misremembered or was not completely familiar with the story, and perhaps that Ó Duilearga was not well acquainted with the local dialect.

Nevertheless, when pieced together the fragments available were reminiscent of other humorous stories where hapless fishermen are offered their heart's desire by some otherworldly entity only to choose something less extravagant but eminently practical (see Irish Folk Tales of Coast and Sea, The History Press, 2024 – 'The Cape Clear Fisherman').

In my attempt to make something of the story, I couldn't help focusing on the querulous wife's apparent wish to be a queen and imagining an ending where the joke was on her.

Many long years ago, there was a poor hapless fisherman who lived in a tiny hovel with his ill-humoured wife on Rathlin Island. They were barely able to keep themselves alive with what little the fisherman could bring home. In the summertime life was hard and hunger was never far from their door. In the winter or when the weather was bad they would go for days living off only what could be scraped from the rocks or found along the shore.

Day after day, when the sea allowed, the fisherman set sail in his little worn-out currach. Sometimes he was lucky but oftentimes not. Time and again it was that he pleaded to whatever gods of the sea were listening that he might at least hook one fish and have something to take home to his ever-complaining wife.

One day the fisherman went way out off the island, farther than he had ever gone before. The sea was calm, but the water was deep. Down, down his line went and then suddenly he felt a jig playing on his hook. Hand over hand, he pulled the line up through the water. What kind of a fish it was the fisherman did not know, but it was putting up a quare fight, for he was barely able to bring it to the surface, so lively was it. Still and all, he stuck to his task and eventually the fisherman saw flashes of silver here and there as the fish played dash back and forth through the upper waters.

Although the fisherman had never done well for himself at sea, over the years he had caught herring and mackerel and haddock and cod, and a great number of other fish, too many to name here. One fish he had never caught was the salmon, for there are no rivers on Rathlin and he was not lucky enough to catch one in the sea. Now, though, on his line was great big shimmering bar of silver. It was 50lb in weight if it was an ounce. Truth be told, it was nearly too big for the wee currach, and the fisherman greatly feared the fish would sink him. Nonetheless, in his excitement he managed to board the salmon with just enough to-do.

As he sat there staring at the mighty fish, a grand big smile spread across his face, for this salmon would fetch a good sum of money. But then the strangest thing happened. The fish spoke to him!

'Put me back in the sea,' it said. 'And I will grant you anything your heart desires.'

As you might imagine, the fisherman was greatly taken aback by this turn of events. He thought for a moment or two that maybe with all his efforts he had become feverish.

'I am the king of the fish,' said the salmon. 'I have powers beyond your imagination. Return me and you will have whatever you wish for.'

'Anything I wish for?' said the fisherman.

'Anything, but mind I am drowning here, so be quick,' said the salmon urgently.

'Very good,' said the fisherman. 'I wish for a fine big, whitewashed, stone-built house overlooking Church Bay and an acre or two of land to grow a spud. That's what I've dreamed of my whole life.'

'So it will be. Now put me back in the sea before I die,' cried the salmon.

Well, there were more comings and goings, but that was the gist of it. To cut a long story short, the fisherman put the king of the fish back into the sea, though it pained him greatly to do so, for he had never caught such a fine specimen before. With that he turned his currach and made for home, wondering all the way if the fish had played him for a fool.

As he neared the shore, the fisherman could see a fine big, whitewashed, stone-built house overlooking the bay, and it freshly thatched. Outside was his wife waiting impatiently. She was still in the rags he had left her that morning, but the house looked grand.

It took the fisherman a bit of time to explain to his wife what had taken place between him and the king of the fish, for she kept interrupting to ask this or that. Eventually, though, he told her all there was to tell. There was a long silence and then the ranting and raving started.

'You're such a gull of a man,' his wife said. 'You could have wished for anything in the whole world that you wanted.'

'Sure, I did,' replied the fisherman.

'But you could have wished,' she screamed in exasperation, 'that … that … I was a queen! But no, you only thought to wish for a wee bit of a house. God's luck to your wit, for you have but little. You'll go back out there tomorrow and find that fish and I'll go with you. You'll tell him you want to make another wish!'

Well, the next day there was a bit of storm, but the fisherman's wife insisted he would go back out to sea, and she went with him. And didn't he catch the same fish again?

'I didn't expect you back here again,' said the fish. 'What troubles you?'

'It's my wife here,' said the fisherman shyly. 'She's not happy with the wish I made.'

'Not happy? For why is she not happy?'

'She said I could have wished for her to be a queen.'

'And sure so you could have, but is this really what you want?' asked the salmon.

'That's what she says,' declared the fisherman, and his wife duly smiled and nodded her agreement.

'Well in that case, so be it,' said the king of the fish. 'I have many queens but one more will make no difference.'

There was a blinding flash and just by that wasn't the fisherman's wife transformed into a big hen salmon flapping her tail in the bottom of the currach.

'Now put us both into the sea,' said the salmon, and the fisherman heeled them both over the side, and as he did so he bid his wife a fond farewell and good luck.

They say the fisherman lived quite happily in his fine house overlooking the bay and spent the rest of his days growing spuds and catching a few fish on calm days as he needed. As for his wife, he never saw her again, but hoped she was happy as a queen – of the fishes.

45. The Last Fox

Michael J. Murphy collected this scrap of folklore on Rathlin Island. It is in his book, Now You're Talking, Folktales from the North of Ireland *(Blackstaff Press Ltd, 1975), written down as he remembered hearing it. It consists of only a few sentences and perhaps that's all it warrants. I couldn't help expanding it slightly in the hope of providing a slightly better overall picture.*

Incidentally, today a great effort is well under way to rid Rathlin of both brown rats and feral ferrets. In years gone by it was believed throughout Dál Riada that rodents especially could be got rid of by the simple expedient of mocking them in verse or commanding them to leave by instructions written in rhyme. Such a lot of effort and expense could have been saved if those currently involved in vermin control on Rathlin had known this!

It is interesting to speculate if stories will be told about this episode of island history in years to come – I suspect not.

For many a day it has been well known that Rathlin is bereft of foxes, and so the islanders could let their fowl roam free without too much concern. It wasn't always so, for foxes once dwelt among the gnarly woods and rocky glens of that little isle.

Being a fairly small place, however, once the islanders began to persecute their native foxes it didn't take long to rid the place of their unwelcome presence. Soon the population was reduced to only one wily old vixen. To shun her human tormentors, she took to scavenging along the shore at night and sleeping in sea caves by day.

One evening at low tide she was hunting limpets by sneaking up quietly and dislodging them before they could take a good grip on the rock on which they lived. At last, the fox came across a great big limpet – the biggest she'd ever seen. 'This will make a tasty bite,' thought the fox as she crept up on her lowly prey.

She quickly slipped her tongue underneath the shell, as she did with all her limpet victims who, unable to then make a tight seal, were easily prized off their rock by the fox's sharp teeth. This limpet, however, was so large that it clamped itself to the surface of the basalt with such strength that it trapped the fox's tongue. Try as she might, the poor vixen could not free herself, and the limpet held fast. The more she struggled, the more it held on for grim death. And a grim death it was, for as the ebb tide swept in, the fox was drowned. That vixen was the last of her kind, and never again was the eerie call of the fox heard on Rathlin Island.

NORTH ANTRIM AND THE GLENS

46. The Hireling Girl

The motif of a mortal invited into the faerie realm as a helper and permitted to leave, but with a dire warning that he or she must never recognise the faeries if they should ever meet again, and who is subsequently blinded for doing so, appears in numerous stories. The story of the Faerie Midwife, for example, which features in numerous volumes, comes most readily to mind (see further reading).

Likewise, the existence of an enchanted isle is very common in the folklore of Dál Riada and beyond. Variously referred to as The Blest or Blessed Isle, The Green Isle, Hy Brasil and Tír na nÓg, it was said to only appear every seven years and almost always situated somewhere out in the Western Ocean.

The following was rendered out of material also collected by Murphy from Rose McCurdy of Rathlin Island in 1956, and appears in his book Now You're Talking, Folktales from the North of Ireland. *A version can also be found in the Irish National Folklore Collection (NFC), 1365, pp.136–137.*

Murphy's recording seems to be two separate sketches under the one title, 'The Enchanted Isle', and I have blended them together.

The town of Ballycastle on the north coast of Antrim is most famous for the Oul Lammas Fair, which even yet people flock to every August. In years gone by the most important fairs were held on the second Tuesdays of May and November – the gale days when the rent was paid to landlords and farmers gathered to hire young boys and girls as cowherds and housemaids. Those hired were bound to their new masters, good or bad, for six months.

It was at the November Hiring Fair that a young peasant girl, no more than 14 years old and even more unworldly than others her age, was hired by a gentleman farmer. He offered her a golden guinea, a sum far beyond the few shillings she might have hoped for at best.

'You will stay with me for a year,' he said.

The girl nodded her agreement, for the offer was too good to refuse.

As was the custom and to seal the bargain, she handed him her bundle – a tied-up parcel of tattered cloth that contained her few worldly possessions. Her new master was plainly dressed. He wore a long dark cloak, and a broad-brimmed hat pulled down over his brow. He was a man of very few words, but he had an air about him that told the girl he was kindly enough. He bid her to follow him up a narrow street away from the clamour of the fair in the Diamond and showed her to a fine white horse that was waiting.

He helped her up onto the animal's back behind him and by the time they got away outside the town it was coming on dark. The girl was surprised when the gentleman reined in the horse and brought it to a halt. He took a silken hood from somewhere under his cloak and made to place over the girl's head, but she shied away.

'Fear not, child,' said he. 'I mean you no harm. Wear this until we arrive at our journey's end, for I want no one to know the way to my dwelling.'

The gentleman spoke so soothingly that the girl agreed and pulled the garment over her head, and on they travelled. After what seemed like an eternity, during which the girl had drifted off to sleep and wakened many times, she heard the gentleman call 'Whoa,' and the horse came to a halt once more.

'You can take off the hood now,' said her employer, and though the girl did so still she could see nothing but darkness.

Soon the gentleman had lamps lighted and a fire blazing away on the hearth, and the girl was able to look about her. His house was well kept for a man who seemingly lived by himself. The furniture and fixings were more comfortable and grander than anything she had ever seen in her short and simple life. Her own quarters were so charming and lovely that she could not stop smiling for sheer joy.

The next morning the gentleman put her to work. It was nothing she hadn't done before, nor was it overly tiring: collecting the eggs and milking the cow, rekindling the fire and making the master's breakfast.

The days passed happily enough for the young girl. Never a complaint had she about her master, nor he about her. Content as she was, she never noticed the time slipping by at all, except in the rare moments when she thought on her family. Then her heart would ache, and she longed to see her mother again.

One morning, however, the gentleman called her.

'Your time here is coming to an end,' he said, 'but if you wish to stay I would be willing to pay you another gold guinea.'

'Thank you sir,' said the girl politely. 'You have been good to me, but I would like to go home to see my mother.'

'I will be sorry to lose you,' he said sharply. 'We will leave in the morning.'

With that the girl went back to her chores, though her thoughts were now of home. She was sad to think on leaving her master, so well had he treated her, but she had been away from family and friends long enough. She knew her mother would be impatient to see her again. Not a word had she heard of her family, for the master forbade any correspondence with the outside world. Only now did the girl begin to think it strange that she had never seen another living soul in all her time with the gentleman. Strange it was too that her master never seemed to want for anything, and that the sky was always blue and the trees always green.

The following morning the gentleman called his servant girl early. He paid her the golden guinea, and in the farmyard he had his horse ready. Again, he asked her gently to place the hood over her head. This time the girl agreed happily, so trusting had she become of the gentleman. And this time she was so excited at the prospect of going home she was awake to every jolt of the horse and every breath of the breeze. She soon heard seagulls crying and waves crashing. She smelled the freshness of the salt sea and through the fine cloth tasted it on her lips. After a while she heard the familiar song of the robin and realised she had not heard them around her master's farm. The fresh smell of earth and green grass began to fill her nose and soon the gentleman called 'Whoa,' and brought his horse to a halt.

'You can take off the hood now,' he said.

As she did so her eyes took in the familiar countryside outside the town of Ballycastle, though everything looked older, and the hedges overgrown. It was late autumn time again. The leaves were brown and piled up along the roadsides, and the wind was cold.

'I will leave you here,' he said solemnly. 'Be warned, if ever you should lay eyes on me again, do not speak nor even pretend to know me. It will not go well for you if you do.'

With that the gentleman galloped away and left the girl to walk the few miles back into Ballycastle. She was vexed at her master's parting gift and shed more than few tears, for she had believed he thought more of her than that. When she eventually came to her mother's dwelling, the woman shrieked as if she had seen a ghost.

'Dear God! Is it really you? Where in the world have you been all these years, girl?' said her mother as she squeezed her daughter's flesh to make sure she was not dead.

'All these years?' said the girl, 'I have been hired this last twelve months mother.'

The girl tossed the golden guinea down onto the table as proof of her endeavours.

It took the girl's mother a long time to convince her daughter that she had been away for seven years, that everyone had believed her dead, and that they had even held a wake for her. When the girl told her story, those who knew best said she had been hired by one of the faerie folk and taken away to the Green Isle – an enchanted otherworldly place far over the waves that only took form every seven years. No good would come of it, they said. But the girl's mother was glad to have her daughter back, and more than happy to take the golden guinea – faerie money or no.

And that would have been the end of the story, except that at the next hiring fair the girl was there. Long had she thought on her employer and how he had played her for a fool. And then suddenly, in among the crowds of hawkers and card-trick men and farmers and dealers she saw the gentleman who had hired her. He was dressed as before with his long woollen cloak and hat. He walked through the throng as if he saw no one and the people paid him not the slightest bit of notice.

Breathlessly the girl pushed her way through the people. Eventually she came within hailing distance and called to the gentleman.

'Sir. Sir, wait!' she cried. 'It's me, do you not remember? You hired me for a year – or was it for seven years?'

At that the gentleman turned. For the first time the girl saw rage in his eyes.

'I warned you never to speak to me again did I not?' he said bitterly.

Before the girl could answer he raised the folds of his great cloak and swept them across her face violently. She fell down in the street as if dead. When she recovered herself, the poor girl had lost the sight of both eyes. She never saw a pin of daylight again. Those who knew best always said that no good ever came from any dealings with the faerie folk.

47. A Bark from Beyond

Throughout Dál Riada there are countless stories of faerie dogs and other strange and faithful hounds, some of whom I have already introduced. Fathers, mothers, sea captains and many other human ghosts have returned from the grave to help their children, crewmates or friends. I have not come across many stories, however, that feature a hound returning from beyond the veil to assist its erstwhile master.

I discovered this lovely little sketch in Jeanne Cooper Foster's Ulster Folklife. *It was told to her nearly a century ago by a farmer in North Antrim, who claimed it had happened to him! I could not resist interpreting it as a folk tale, incorporating images of the bog from my own experience and other folkloric elements.*

What remains of the once vast Garry Bog lies to the west of the River Bush just north of Ballymoney. It is representative of one of the largest remaining areas of uncut lowland raised bog in the north of Ireland and is designated an Area of Special Scientific Interest.

The beautiful Garry Bog in North Antrim was once a mystifying wilderness. Its dark, watery depths still hide secrets and treasures from the past that many are yet trying to uncover. There are countless moss holes – dangerous bottomless pools and quagmires – that have swallowed many an unwary traveller, be they two-legged or four. There were even stories of evil doings and bog bodies.

And yet to be out in the bog on a night in late spring when the cuckoo and the curlew are calling their own names and the snipe are bleating overhead is a magical thing. Hares and foxes abound, and their well-trodden trails criss-cross the landscape. To follow these through the heather, the traveller would be well advised, but even by daylight the way is easily lost. The bog with its many moods is a dangerous place in which to be caught out.

Just such a thing happened to a local man one May evening long ago. Coming home late, he had taken a shortcut across the moss, as local people call the bog due to the abundance of sphagnum and other mossy, bog-loving plants. The man thought he knew the Garry Bog well, for he had lived beside it all his life, but his decision was a careless one.

First a mist settled like a blanket over the heather. Rising only to knee height and so dense that the man could not see where to place his feet, he was unable to go forward or back with any measure of faith. The bird calls fell away, and the layer of mist slowly rose to head height and blocked out even a glimmer of the stars. The walking became easier, but the eerie sensation of that cold shroud just overhead would have rattled the nerves even of the most dauntless. The man had heard the old folk tell stories of the bog faeries luring people away with their wee wispy lights. He began to fear for himself and imagine things like faraway voices and distant laughing. He became hopelessly lost and confused.

Even in springtime it was perishing when the cold mist came down, and to stray into a moss hole would mean a cold and watery end. No one would ever find him. Standing there in the darkness wondering what he should do, the bark of a dog suddenly rent the night. It was a strangely familiar sound. The bark came again, but closer this time, and it sent shivers down the man's spine for no dwelling house was near. Then he became aware of the presence of a dog. It seemed friendly enough and he even felt the comforting cold damp of its nose as it touched his hand briefly.

The dog moved on and instinctively the man followed, carefully feeling the ground with each step but slowly gaining confidence. He talked to the dog encouragingly, as much to cheer himself as spur it on. At times he could hardly see the dog, but he could feel it was there guiding him every step of the way.

The man followed the dog until it brought him to more solid and familiar ground. The mist had already cleared, and he was now able to find his own way. He got one last glimpse of the animal in the moonlight reflecting off a bog pool by the side of the path. It was then he realised that it was his own long-dead and much-loved collie dog that had come from beyond the grave to guide its master one last time.

Its spirit departed, the man believed his faithful dog returned to the grave in which he had buried it in the bog, and over which he whispered, 'Lie easy old friend, we will meet again.' And that's a true story, for it was the man who told it himself.

48. The Breed of the Old Mare

I found this story in Murphy's Now You're Talking, Folktales from the North of Ireland. *Set and collected in the Glens of Antrim, it centres around the same motif as that found in the Skye story 'A Rare Breed'. The emphasis and ending here, however, are markedly different, which, in my view, warranted a rendering of both.*

Whether the teller here was not familiar with a more comprehensive version like that from Skye and foreshortened it with his own ending is impossible to know. Similar versions exist where, for example, the victim's brother stands in for him (see Scottish Fairy and Folk Tales, *Sir George Douglas, A.L. Burt Company, New York, 1901). It is interesting to note how certain stories seem to have become widespread throughout the region, but also how they vary from teller to teller.*

It was very many years ago in the Glens of Antrim – Glencloy they say it was – that a young cub was hired to a woman away up over the mountains near Loughguile. She was no spring chicken, but she had most of her own teeth and her hair was far from grey. The young fellow was always thought of as a hard worker, but he wasn't long in with the woman 'til he was rising late and was not fit to get on with his chores. It was the same every morning. He would rise more tired than when he went to his bed and by next bedtime he was dropping off his feet with tiredness.

After a while this began to concern him greatly and eventually he went to an old man they said had the gift of wisdom and charms. When the old man had listened to the lad's tale of trouble, he never spoke for a while.

'I think,' said he eventually, 'you've been hired by some class of a witch.'

'A witch!' cried the young fellow in despair.

'Oh aye, I've seen it all before,' said the old man. 'While you're sleeping she'll whisper a charm over ye and turn ye into a wee horse. Then she'll ride ye all over the Glens of Antrim at whatever mischief she's up to.'

Well, the young fellow was lost for the power of speech, for he'd never in his young life heard of the likes before and the old man put the fear of God into him.

'Here's what you need to do young fella,' said the old man reassuringly. 'Lie down the night and whatever ye do don't sleep nor let on you're awake. When she performs her spell, jump you up and repeat the very same words back to her as quick as ye can, and ye will see what ye will see.'

Night-time came and the young fellow got ready for bed. He lay down in the blankets and let on to be asleep. In came his mistress as the old man had foretold. In a low voice she began to recite a few lines of whimsical verse.

'Sleep the night ye ne'er will get,
'For we have work unholy yet
'To undertake before the morn.
'Rise ye now a steed unborn.'

The young fellow listened carefully, though he didn't understand what her words meant. When she was finished her wee recitation and was about to strike him with her hazel wand, he bounced out of the bed like a lion. He snatched the hazel wand from her and like lightning turned the spell back upon her.

'Sleep the night ye ne'er will get,
'For we have work unholy yet

'To undertake before the morn.
'Rise ye now a steed unborn.'

Immediately he spoke the words, he struck her with the wand as if he was some class of a druid, and low and behold didn't she transform there and then into a fine wee chestnut mare. In an instant the young fellow mounted her and away he galloped all over the Glens of Antrim. By dawn he was spent, and the mare was frothing at the mouth and her coat glistened with sweat.

What the old wise man did not tell the young fellow was how to turn her from a horse back into a woman. Thus, he had no choice but to let her go and fend for herself as a wee wild mare. Around the Glens of Antrim, they will still swear to it that breed of the mare is up about Loughguile yet.

49. The Farmer, the Henwife and the Hare

This is a very well-known story plot in the Glens of Antrim and many other places. To have the 'blink' put on milking cows or other animals or, more generally, a farmer's luck, was a common superstition or 'pishogue' up until relatively recent times. The phrase 'to be on the blink' has passed into modern parlance to mean something that is not working as it should – 'that car is on the blink again'.

The motif of the hare-woman or hare-witch appears in many folk tales across the islands of Ireland and Britain. Sometimes she is mischievous but kindly, and at others a more malign character.

This story is adapted from a slightly more convoluted version found in Jack McBride's Traveller in the Glens *(Appletree Press, 1979), and other sources.*

There was once a hard-working farmer in the Glens of Antrim who was in a good way of going. He had half a dozen fine wee cows that gave his wife the creamiest of milk. In turn she made butter by the stone and the folk came from far and wide to deal for it. Forby this they kept a dozen hens that laid the best of good eggs.

Well, the hard-working farmer had a neighbour who was as lazy as sheugh water. He only had one old bow-backed cow, and the ribs could be counted along its flank, for it was only a rickle of bones. He only had two or three old hens with hardly a feather on them and they looked as if their next egg would be their last.

But then one time the hard-working farmer's cows all dried up. Almost overnight they went from gallons of cream a day to a dribble of sour slop that even the pigs would have turned their noses up at. If this was not bad enough, his flock of hens went off the lay, and not an egg for baking nor breakfast did they yield. Funnily enough, the hard-working farmer began to notice that his lazy neighbour seemed to be thriving. The folk were coming from far and wide to deal with his wife for butter and milk and eggs.

The hard-working farmer began to imagine that his neighbours were up to something. When weeks went by and his suspicions became a matter of certainty, he decided that he would have to pay a visit to an old wise woman – a henwife who was known to be well-versed in matters of magic and dark practices. The old woman listen intently as the hard-working farmer relayed his tale of woe.

'What can I do at all?' he cried. 'I'll be brought to beggary if this goes on much longer.'

'There's more to this than meets the eye,' said the henwife very thoughtfully. 'I will come tomorrow and see for myself. Go home now and sleep well.'

The following morning the henwife came as she had promised. She cast her eye over barn and byre, down into the well and all around the place. As she did so she caught the glimpse of a woman watching her through the thorn hedge from the neighbouring farm. It was the lazy farmer's wife. At that the old henwife shivered inwardly.

'I think we have found the cause of your troubles,' she said to the hard-working farmer.

'What's that?' he asked anxiously.

'Someone has put the blink on your cows and your hens. Tonight, we will keep a watch, and we will see what we will see,' she said.

That night the hard-working farmer and the henwife sat up in the old byre where his cows were stalled. Hours passed in silence but eventually they heard a rustling at the door. Both tensed up at the faint sound. And then by the light of the moon, they saw a creature creep in. It was a big hare with its ears and nose twitching nervously.

Man and woman watched in awe as the hare went to each and every cow and sniffed at their udders. But then the animal seemed to sense that all was not well. Suddenly it gave a queer shiver before scurrying off towards the door. Quick as lightning, the farmer rose and threw a reaping hook at the hare and caught

it a glancing blow as it made its escape. The creature cried out with a squeal like that of a child in pain before it ran off into the night. It was slowed enough for the hard-working farmer to keep up.

At last, he saw the hare limp into his lazy neighbour's cabin, and with the temper on him he followed without taking a pause. Not far behind him was the old henwife. There by the fire they saw the lazy farmer tending to a gash on his wife's leg. So occupied were the pair that they did not notice that they were being observed. When they did realise, there was little they could do to deny their foul doings.

Neither the hard-working farmer nor the old henwife ever told what was said in yon house that night, but very soon after the lazy farmer and his wife left without a word and were never heard tell of again.

'Bad cess to them,' said the hard-working farmer, and within a very short time his cows were milking once again and the hens laying like mad.

I'm not sure how long that old henwife lived afterwards, but never for the rest of her days did she want for a jug of cream, a pound of butter or a fresh egg.

50. A Shirt Tale

It's not that long ago that marriages were arranged between feuding families and neighbouring farmers keen to settle disputes or strengthen their clans through intermarital bonds. Even when sons and daughters were not betrothed, some parents still liked to act as matchmakers; indeed there were individuals whose services were sought as marriage brokers. Nowadays such doings would be thought of as interfering and controlling.

In the past there were also many charms and remedies, mainly, it must be said, for the use of young women in their attempts to attract a difficult or disinterested suitor. It is less common to be found the other way around.

The following was adapted from a sketch found in McBride's A Traveller in the Glens *and other sources.*

Once upon a very long time ago there was a pretty young girl by the name of Eibhlís who had a powerful liking for a neighbouring young lad called Tom. He was handsome and could have had his pick of all the young girls in the townland, but he did not know it. That was part of his charm and drew Eibhlís to him all the more.

Both Eibhlís and Tom were the only children born to their families, for their fathers had died years before and neither of their mothers had taken another husband. The mothers had been good friends since girlhood, and both could see the way Eibhlís looked at Tom and how he seemed innocently unaware. Poor Eibhlís had tried every flirtatious thing she could think of but, gull that he was, Tom seemed not to notice her amorous advances and he remained, annoyingly, like a brother to her.

The two mothers could see how advantageous a marriage between Eibhlís and Tom would be in bringing their little families closer and they soon put their heads together to solve the problem.

'My daughter has made her feelings clear as spring water,' said Eibhlís' mother.

'Aye, Tom's the hair in the milk,' said his mother. 'I wouldn't want to push him, mind, for fear he'd pull.'

And so it went, back and forth. The two mothers tried hard to come up with a scheme that might bring their children together.

Eventually they both went to an old wise woman, of which there were many in the Glens of Antrim in those days. They explained their difficulty with the greatest delicacy and waited patiently for the old woman to suggest a charm.

'Next wash day,' she said to Tom's mother, 'you must bring one of your son's shirts to Eibhlís – one that's well-worn, mind. Then,' she continued, but addressing Eibhlís' mother this time, 'your daughter must wash the shirt in along with her drawers – a pair that's well-worn, mind. Hang Tom's shirt and Eibhlís' undergarments by the fire to dry and before the night is out the young couple will be brought together.'

Well, they hadn't long to wait before wash day came around and Tom's mother brought one of his old shirts to Eibhlís for her to wash along with her unmentionables. At first the young girl only half-heartedly took part in the foolishness, but the more time went on the more excited about it she got. The washing was hung up to dry by the fire and Eibhlís waited eagerly to see what might occur.

The hours passed slowly and Eibhlís' mother went on to her bed, but when the moon was high in the sky there came a faint knock to the door. Eibhlís bounced out of her chair near the fire and rubbed the sleep from her eyes.

'Come in,' she said sheepishly, and a coy smile of expectation spread across her face, but when the latch lifted, in came an old beggarman dressed in filthy rags.

'Sorry to be so late, daughter. I was to sleep over in your neighbour's byre, but me and him had words,' explained the old man.

'Words! with Tom?' said Eibhlís. 'Sure, Tom wouldn't say boo to a goose.'

'Aye, well, he accused me of stealing his shirt from the washing. Never in my life did I take as much as blade of grass that didn't belong to me. If somebody took his shirt I know it wasn't me.'

Just then the old man's eyes darted to where Tom's shirt and Eibhlís' drawers were hung up before the fire.

'You'll be wanting to sleep in our byre then,' said Eibhlís quickly, trying to distract the old beggarman from his gaze.

'Naw indeed, I think I'll be on my way,' he said wearily, and he made for the door, but then he added over his shoulder. 'I don't know what kind of folk yeese are at all.'

With that the old man slammed the door behind him and went away.

A short time later Tom came to the door, as he sometimes did in the evenings when he had news or was running some errand for his mother.

'Sorry to be so late,' he said as he let himself in and looked to the fire to see if the kettle was on the boil. When he saw his shirt hanging there beside Eibhlís' drawers, his jaw dropped open. Well, to shorten the story, Eibhlís could do nothing but explain herself honestly there and then. A little bashfully, she told Tom about how their mothers and the old wise woman had put her up to such old-fashioned foolery.

'Tomfoolery, I suppose you could call it,' she said.

For his part Tom could do nothing but laugh, though he was badly vexed about accusing the old beggarman in the wrong. Somehow or another, however, now that the matter was set out in plain words, Tom was much more open to Eibhlís' affections and confessed to his own tender feelings. Within a year the pair were married and many a time they had a good laugh at themselves.

Whether you are a believer in the power of these old charms or not, I think it's fair to say that on this occasion the magic worked a treat. In case you're wondering about the old beggarman, the next time he came about the place, Tom made up for any offence he had caused. Let us hope that the beggarman wished the newly-weds well.

51. A Wee Lift

This heartsome little story is found in Murphy's Now You're Talking, Folktales from the North of Ireland, *under the title 'The Man with the Bar of Gold'. It was written down as Murphy remembered it from various County Antrim sources, but a version recorded by him from Pat O'Neill, County Antrim, can also be found in the IFC (1363, p.252).*

I have taken the liberty of changing the gold bar into coins. I have also changed the original title to 'A Wee Lift' – a phrase used in Murphy's version – but also the title given it by County Antrim storyteller Liz Weir MBE, from whom I first heard the story. The term is commonly used in the north of Ireland to mean something uplifting – like a visit from a friend or some other kind deed that imparts a measure of encouragement or inspiration to the recipient.

There was once a farming man living with his wife in the Glens of Antrim. He owned a grand wee parcel of land and at one time was in a good way of going. Their children were grown up and away and somewhere down the road he had lost heart. The daily grind of life had brought him down, and sure we all know what that can be like. Anyway, he let the wee place go and before long the hens went off the lay and the cows dried up. Every farmer knows you can only neglect livestock for so long before you end up with dead stock, and sure that's what started to happen.

'For two pence,' said the farmer, 'I'd pull the door behind me and take the road.'

To where he would have gone, the farmer, nor his wife, never gave any thought, so they just stayed where they were.

One winter's evening when the snow lay thick all around, a knock came to the door. It was unusual enough, for the neighbours had stopped coming around and the dreariness of the place didn't invite men of the road to call looking for work or a bite to eat. Nevertheless, the old couple had never turned anyone away, so they bid whoever it was to come on in. The door creaked open and in stepped an old man dressed in rags and hardly a shoe to his foot.

'God bless you this night,' said the old man glancing over at the half-dead fire on the hearth. 'Could you spare a wee bite of meat for a weary travelling man?'

'You welcome to share what little we have,' said the farmer's wife, and she poked the remains of the fire and tried to heat the kettle.

As the *tae* was poured out and slices of stale bread handed around, the old man began chatting and telling stories, but he could sense there wasn't much of a desire for mirth.

'I can see you're down on your luck,' he said eventually.

'Aye, we are indeed,' sighed the farmer. 'Sure if it wasn't for bad luck we'd have no luck at all. The truth is, I just can't seem to shake meself.'

'Well,' said the old man, smiling, 'I just might be able to help you turn things around.'

With that he reached inside his coat pocket and pulled out a wee leather purse. He tugged the drawstring on it and out tumbled a handful of bright gold coins, the like of which the farmer nor his wife had ever seen, not even when they were in a good way of going.

'Take these,' said the old man. 'Use what you need to get yourselves back on your feet and sure whatever's left I'll call back for some time again.'

The bag of gold was stowed away in a wee nook up inside the chimney breast and the farmer and his wife were overcome with joy. They both thanked the old man a dozen times for his kindness and promised to use the gold wisely. They insisted he stay for the night at least, and in the morning they shared what breakfast they had with him. Afterwards the old man said he had to go, and took his leave of the farmer and his wife. But for the gold, he never left a trace of his presence – not a whisper nor even a footprint in the snow.

That morning, though, the farmer and his wife took great heart again. Everything they laid their hands to seemed to fall into place. Over the weeks and months, they tidied the wee place up. New curtains were hung and the floor swept clean. Hinges and hedges were mended, byres were cleared out and the midden piled high. Weeds were cut and hay was made, and by the harvest time the fruits of their labours were plentiful and plain to be seen.

That winter the turf was well dried and stacked at the gable end of the house, and the fire burned brightly. One snowy night a knock came to the door and the latch lifted. It was the old man once again.

'I hardly recognised the wee place, it's that well mended up,' said he as he came in.

Again, he was treated to a supper, but this time it was fresh bread and butter and jam and soda farls and wee sweet cakes. When he had eaten his fill, the woman called him up to the blazing fire and he was handed a wee dram of whiskey.

'I see,' said he, 'that you've put the gold I gave to good use.'

'To tell you the truth,' said the farmer, glancing wryly over at his wife, 'since the day and hour I set it up inside that nook in the chimney we haven't looked near it, for in truth we didn't need it.'

'You haven't spent any of the gold?' asked the old man, almost disbelieving.

'Not a penny, sir. All we needed was a wee lift and sure we got that from your kindness,' said the farmer, and he reached up inside the chimney breast and took down the purse.

He tugged the drawstring on it and out tumbled the bright gold coins into the palm of his hand.

'Well, if you don't mind,' said the old man, 'I'll take them back again. Tomorrow I'll be on my way, for you just never know who else might be in need of a wee lift.'

52. A Viking Legacy

The following is a compilation from various sources, two of which are vignettes also found in Murphy's Now You're Talking: Folktales from the North of Ireland *('A Wild Day on the Braes of Layde' and 'The Danes Own All Ireland', as told by Frank McAuley from County Antrim).*

These types of yarn seem to be common in the north of Ireland, and always involve a character from, for example, Norway, who claims intimate knowledge of a local townland or farm in County Antrim (for an unusual version see The Man Who Talked To The Wind, *and other stories from the Tommy Cecil Archive,* The History Press, 2024*). Sometimes, as this story reveals, the knowledge possessed includes the whereabouts of a hoard of buried treasure left by fleeing Vikings.*

It is often said that at one time the Vikings owned all of Ireland. Whatever way it was, after the Battle of Clontarf in 1014 their grip on the Emerald Isle was weakened. In the years that followed, the Norsemen were driven northwards back into the sea from where they came.

Years later, a young sea captain from Cushendall in the Glens of Antrim had occasion to put into a fjord in Norway to collect spars for his ship. While there he got talking to an old local man.

'From what part of Ireland do you come?' said the Norseman.

'You will likely not have heard of it,' said the sea captain. 'It is a little village called Cushendall in the Glens of Antrim, and it is there I wish I was now instead of ploughing the seas trying to make my living.'

'Ah, Cushendall,' said the Norseman. 'The wind will be wild around Layde tonight.'

'You know Cushendall?' asked the sea captain in disbelief.

'Yes, many a night have I dreamed of my fields around Layde, for I heard the stories about them from my father when I was a child,' said the old Norwegian.

'You own land around the townland of Layde?'

'Yes, of course I do.'

'Did your father buy it?' asked the sea captain, trying to make sense of it all.

'No. It was bequeathed him by my grandfather.'

'Ah, I see,' said the Cushendall man. 'So your grandfather must have bought it then.'

'No. It was bequeathed him by his father and by his father before him.'

'I do not understand,' said the sea captain at last.

'My forefathers have not set foot in Ireland for many years,' said the Norseman. 'They were forced to flee their farms long ago, but for many generations our land has been passed down from father to son.'

'Very good,' said the sea captain, laughing now. 'I have heard many a good yarn in my time, but that is the best in a long while.'

'Tell me, do you know Tievebulliagh?' asked the old Norseman very seriously.

'I do,' came back the answer.

'There are rocks found there that ring like a bell and that were once fashioned into the finest polished stone axes, are there not?'

'That is true,' said the sea captain. 'I have seen a few of them.'

'On the north flank of Tievebulliagh there is a spring, is there not?'

'Many a time I quenched my thirst from it,' answered the sea captain.

'Well, I am an old man now and I have no sons, so I am going to tell you something that may be of interest to you. Just beside that spring there is a large flat stone. Underneath that stone is buried a hoard of gold left behind by my ancestors when they fled. Find it and all will be yours.'

Well, as might be imagined, the sea captain took all this with a large pinch of salt. Nevertheless, when he arrived home he climbed up the slopes of Tievebulliagh and found the stone by the spring. With a crowbar, he moved the slab of basalt and then dug a hole down into the earth. In it he found a treasure trove just as the old Norseman had told him.

They say that's how the Cushendall sea captain was able to retire a young man and still live a life of quiet comfort for the rest of his days.

Bibliography

Antrim, Angela, *The Antrim McDonnells*, Ulster Television Publication, 1977.

Boyd, Halbert J., *Strange Tales of the Western Isles*, Eanas McKay, Stirling, 1930.

Campbell, J.F., *Popular Tales of the West Highlands, (4 Volumes)*, Edmonston and Douglas of Edinburgh, 1860.

Campbell, Lord Archibald, *Waifs and Strays of the Celtic Tradition, Argyll Series (5 volumes)*, David Nutt, London, 1889–95.

Douglas, Sir George, *Scottish Fairy and Folk Tales*, A.L. Burt Company, New York, 1901.

Foster, Jeanne Cooper, *Ulster Folklore*, H.R. Carter Publications Ltd, Belfast, 1951.

Gregorson Campbell, John, *Superstitions of the Highlands and Islands of Scotland*, James MacLehose and Sons, Glasgow, 1900.

Grice, F., *Folktales of the North Country*, Thomas Nelson & Sons Ltd, 1946.

Jacobs, Joseph, *Celtic Fairy Tales*, David Nutt, London, 1892.

Kirk, Robert, *The Secret Commonwealth of Elves, Fauns and Fairies*, London, Andrew Lang, 1893.

Lupton, Hugh, *Tales of Wisdom and Wonder*, Barefoot Books Ltd, 2000.

MacClean, Fitzroy, *West Highland Tales*, William Collins and Company Limited, 1985.

MacCulloch, J.A., *The Misty Isle of Skye Oliphant*, Anderson & Ferrier, Edinburgh and London, 1905.

McCully, Madeline, *Haunted Antrim*, The History Press, 2017.

MacDonald, David, *Running with the Fox*, Unwin Hyman, 1987.

McBride Jack, *Traveller in the Glens*, Appletree Press, 1979.

McClean, J.P., *History of the Clan McClean*, Robert Clarke & Co., Cincinnati, 1889.

McCurdy, Augustine, *Stories and Legends of Rathlin*, privately printed, 2006.

McGregor, Alisdair Alpin, *The Peat Fire Flame*, The Moray Press, Edinburgh & London, 1937.

Muir, Tom, *Tales of Viking Lands*, Orcadian Ltd, 2014.

Murphy, Michael J., *Now You're Talking*, Blackstaff Press, Belfast, 1975.

Power, Patrick C., *The Book of Irish Curses*, The Mercier Press, Dublin and Cork, 1974.

Swire, Otto F., *The Inner Hebrides and their Legends*, Collins, London and Glasgow, 1964.

Swire, Otto F., *Skye, The Island and its Legends*, Blackie & Son Limited, Glasgow, 1961.

Urwin, Colin, *The Iron Hag and Other Stories from the Sam Henry Collection*, Causeway Museum Service, 2023.

Urwin, Colin, *Irish Folk Tales of Coast and Sea*, The History Press, 2024.

Urwin, Colin, *The Man Who Talked To The Wind and Other Rathlin Folk Tales from the Tommy Cecil Archive*, The History Press, 2024

Wilde, Lady Francesca Speranza, *Ancient Legends, Mystic Charms and Superstitions of Ireland*, Ward and Downey, London, 1888.

Williamson, Duncan and Linda, *The Genie and the Fisherman*, Cambridge University Press, 1991.